Isaac Lea, Temple Prime, William Stimpson, Institution Smithsonian, William G. Binney, Philip P. Carpenter

Check Lists of the Shells of North America

Isaac Lea, Temple Prime, William Stimpson, Institution Smithsonian, William G. Binney, Philip P. Carpenter

Check Lists of the Shells of North America

ISBN/EAN: 9783337387112

Printed in Europe, USA, Canada, Australia, Japan

Cover: Foto ©Andreas Hilbeck / pixelio.de

More available books at **www.hansebooks.com**

SMITHSONIAN MISCELLANEOUS COLLECTIONS.

CHECK LISTS

OF THE

SHELLS OF NORTH AMERICA.

PREPARED FOR THE SMITHSONIAN INSTITUTION,

BY

**ISAAC LEA, P. P. CARPENTER, WM. STIMPSON,
W. G. BINNEY, AND TEMPLE PRIME.**

WASHINGTON:
SMITHSONIAN INSTITUTION.
JUNE, 1860.

PHILADELPHIA:

COLLINS, PRINTER, 705 JAYNE STREET.

INTRODUCTION.

THE following lists of the described species of North American shells have been prepared at the request of this Institution, by several accomplished conchologists, for the purpose of labelling the specimens in the Smithsonian collection.

Applications having been made for copies of the lists, it has been though that their publication would be generally useful, in facilitating the pre paration of catalogues, the labelling of collections, conducting exchanges, checking off faunas of particular regions, etc.

The series of lists is complete with the exception of that of the marine fauna of the West India Province, including the shores of Florida, the Gulf coast, the West Indies, etc. On account of the great extent of this province, and the uncertainty in relation to many of its species, together with their imperfect representation in American conchological collections, it has been thought expedient to omit for the present a list of its shells. As soon as such a list can be properly prepared, it will be added to the series.

In accordance with the views of a majority of the compilers of the lists, the authority given for each name refers to the original describer of the species, and not to the one who first published the name, both generic and specific, as here printed.

It will be readily understood that the Smithsonian Institution cannot vouch for the accuracy of the names of the lists or for their completeness, and that all responsibility in reference to these points rests with the several authors.

JOSEPH HENRY,
Secretary S. I.

SMITHSONIAN INSTITUTION,
May, 1860.

TABLE OF CONTENTS.

CHECK LIST

OF THE

SHELLS OF NORTH AMERICA.

WEST COAST:

OREGONIAN AND CALIFORNIAN PROVINCE.

BY

P. P. CARPENTER.

THIS list is condensed from that presented in the "Report to the British Association," 1856, pp. 298 *et seq.* Species are omitted which have since been discovered to be synonyms, or which rest on doubtful authority as occurring in this zoological province; which is known to extend from Puget Sound to San Diego. Stragglers from other districts are omitted; as also the species peculiar to the peninsula of Lower California.

The generic names alone are given of undescribed species in the Smithsonian collection, or of species not yet satisfactorily identified.

PALLIOBRANCHIATA.
Discinidæ.
1. Discina Evansii, *Dav.*
Terebratulidæ.
2. Waldheimia californica, *Koch.*
3. Terebratella caurina, *Gld.*
4. Terebratella pulvinata, *Gld.*

LAMELLIBRANCHIATA.
Pholadidæ.
5. Teredo
6. Zirphæa ?crispata, *Linn.*
7. Pholadidea ovoidea, *Gld.*
8. Pholadidea penita, *Conr.*
9. Parapholas californica, *Conr.*
Saxicavidæ.
10. Saxicava pholadis, *Lam.*
Myidæ.
11. Panopæa generosa, *Gld.*
12. Mya præcisa, *Gld.*
13. Platyodon cancellata, *Conr.*
14. Cryptomya californica, *Conr.*
15. Tresus capax, *Gld.*
16. Schizothoerus Nuttallii, *Conr.*

Corbulidæ.
17. Neæra
18. Sphænia
Anatinidæ.
19. Thracia curta, *Conr.*
20. Lyonsia californica, *Conr.*
21. Mytilimeria Nuttallii, *Conr.*
22. Periploma argentaria, *Conr.*
23. Pandora punctata, *Conr.*
24. Pandora
Solenidæ.
25. Solen sicarius, *Gld.*
Solecurtidæ.
26. Machæra lucida, *Conr.*
27. Machæra patula, *Port.*
28. Solecurtus californianus, *Conr.*
29. Solecurtus subteres, *Conr.*
Tellinidæ.
30. Sanguinolaria Nuttallii, *Conr.*
31. Sanguinolaria rubroradiata, *C*
32. Psammobia pacifica, *Conr.*
33. Tellina bodegensis, *Hds.*
34. Tellina
35. Tellina

(a)

36. Tellina
37. Tellina
38. Macoma edulis, *Nutt.*
39. Macoma inconspicua, *B. & Sby.*
40. Macoma nasuta, *Conr.*
41. Macoma secta, *Conr.*
42. Scrobicularia alta, *Conr.*
43. Strigilla carnaria, *Linn.*
44. Semele decisa, *Conr.*
45. Semele rubrolineata, *Conr.*
46. Cumingia californica, *Conr.*

Donacidæ.

47. Donax californicus, *Conr.*
48. Donax flexuosus, *Gld.*
49. Arcopagia vicina, *C. B. Ad.*

Mactridæ.

50. Mactra californica, *Conr.*
51. Mactra falcata, *Gld.*
52. Mactra planulata, *Conr.*

Veneridæ.

53. Trigona crassatelloides, *Conr.*
54. ?Trigona tantilla, *Gld.*
55. Dione callosa, *Conr.*
56. Venus californiensis, *Sby.*
57. Venus dispar.
58. Venus excavata, *Cpr.*
59. Venus fluctifraga, *Sby.*
60. Venus Nuttallii, *Conr.*
61. Venus
62. Tapes gracilis, *Gld.*
63. Tapes Petitii, *Desh.*
64. Tapes rigida, *Gld.*
65. Tapes staminea, *Conr.*

Petricolidæ.

66. Petricola californica, *Conr.*
67. Rupellaria lamellifera, *Conr.*
68. Saxidomus aratus, *Gld.*
69. Saxidomus Nuttallii, *Conr.*

Astartidæ.

70. Astarte
71. Trapezium californicum, *Conr.*
72. Cardita ventricosa, *Gld.*

Chamidæ.

73. Chama exogyra, *Conr.*
74. Chama pellucida, *Rve.*

Cardiadæ.

75. Cardium californiense, *Desh.*
76. Cardium (*like* grœnlandicum).
77. Cardium luteolabrum, *Gld.*
78. Cardium Nuttalli. *Conr.*
79. Cardium quadragenarium, *Con.*
80. Cardium substriatum, *Conr.*

Lucinidæ.

81. Lucina bella, *Conr.*
82. Lucina californica, *Conr.*

83. Lucina Nuttallii, *Conr.*
84. Lucina
85. Cryptodon

Diplodontidæ.

86. Diplodonta orbella, *Gld.*

Kelliadæ.

87. Kellia Laperousii, *Desh.*
88. Kellia [rugifera].
89. Kellia suborbicularis, *Mont.*
90. Lasea
91. Montacuta

Mytilidæ.

92. Mytilus californianus, *Conr*
93. Mytilus edulis, *Linn.*
94. Mytilus glomeratus, *Gld.*
95. Septifer
96. Modiola capax, *Conr.*
97. Modiola elongata, *Swains.*
98. Modiola flabellata, *Gld.*
99. Modiola modiolus. *Linn.*
100. Modiola nitens, *Cpr.*
101. Modiola recta, *Conr.*
102. Modiola
103. Crenella [*like* discrepans].
104. Lithophagus falcatus, *Gld.*
105. Lithophagus

Arcadæ.

106. Arca labiata, *Sby.*
107. Arca ?multicostata, *Sby.*
108. Byssoarca pernoides, *Cpr.*
109. Axinæa septentrionalis, *M.*

Nuculidæ.

110. Nucula cælata, *Hds.*
111. Nucula ?tenuis, *Mont.*
112. Leda ?caudata, *Mont.*
113. Leda
114. Yoldia
115. Yoldia

Pectinidæ.

116. Pecten Fabricii, *Phil.*
117. Pecten hericius, *Gld.*
118. Pecten (*like* Islandicus).
119. Pecten latiauratus, *Conr.*
120. Pecten ?nodosus, *Linn.*
121. Pecten purpuratus, *Lam.*
122. Pecten ?ventricosus, *Sby.*
123. Amusium caurinum, *Gld.*
124. Janeira florida,' *Hds.*
125. Hinnites giganteus, *Gray.*

Ostræidæ.

126. Ostrea conchaphila, *Cpr.*
127. Ostrea [lurida].
128. Ostrea rufa, *Gld.*

Anomiadæ.

129. Placunanomia alope, *Gray.*

130. Placunanomia cepio, *Gray.*
131. Placunanomia macroschisma,
132. Anomia lampe, *Gray.* [*Desh.*

GASTEROPODA OPISTHOBRANCHIATA.
Bullidæ.

133. Bulla nebulosa, *Gld.*
134. Haminea vesicula, *Gld.*
135. Haminea virescens, *Sby.*
136. Haminea
137. Tornatina cerealis, *Gld.*
138. Tornatina culcitella, *Gld.*
139. Tornatina inculta, *Gld.*
140. Tornatina
141. Cylichna

GASTEROPODA PROSOBRANCHIATA.
CIRRIBRANCHIATA.
Dentaliadæ.

142. Dentalium
143. Dentalium

SCUTIBRANCHIATA.
Chitonidæ.

144. Callochiton interstinctus, *Gld.*
145. Lepidochiton Mertensii, *Midd.*
146. Lepidochiton scrobiculatus, *M.*
147. Tonicia lineata, *Wood.*
148. Mopalia Blainvillei, *Brod.*
149. Mopalia Hindsii, *Sby.*
150. Mopalia Simpsonii, *Gray.*
151. Mopalia vespertina, *Gld.*
152. Katherina tunicata, *Sby.*
153. Cryptochiton Stelleri, *Midd.*
154. (Chiton) acutus, *Cpr.*
155. (Chiton) californicus, *Nutt.*
156. (Chiton) dentiens, *Gld.*
157. (Chiton) Hartwegii, *Cpr.*
158. (Chiton) lignosus, *Gld.*
159. (Chiton) montereyensis, *C.*
160. Chiton muscosus, *Gld.*
161. (Chiton) Nuttalli, *Cpr.*
162. (Chiton) ornatus, *Nutt.*
163. (Chiton) regularis, *Cpr.*
164. Chiton scaber, *Rve.*
165. (Chiton) Wosnessenskii, *M.*

Patellidæ.

166. Patella toreuma, *Rve.*
167. Nacella depicta, *Hds.*
168. Nacella incessa, *Hds.*
169. Nacella instabilis, *Gld.*

Acmæidæ.

170. Acmæa Asmi, *Midd.*

171. Acmæa patina, *Esch.*
172. Acmæa pelta, *Esch.*
173. Acmæa persona, *Esch.*
174. Acmæa scabra, *Nutt.*
175. Acmæa spectrum, *Nutt.*
176. [Tecturella] grandis, *Gray.*
177. Scurria mitra, *Esch.*

Fissurellidæ.

178. Fissurella volcano, *Rve.*
179. Glyphis aspera, *Esch.*
180. Lucapina crenulata, *Sby.*
181. Puncturella cucullata, *Gld.*
182. Puncturella galeata, *Gld.*

Haliotidæ.

183. Haliotis californiensis, *Swains.*
184. Haliotis corrugata, *Gray.*
185. Haliotis Cracherodii, *Leach.*
186. Haliotis [*like* kamtschatkiana]
187. Haliotis rufescens, *Swains.*
188. Haliotis splendens, *Rve.*

Trochidæ.

189. Phasianella compta, *Gld.*
190. Pomaulax undosus, *Wood.*
191. Pachypoma diadematum, *Val*
192. Trochiscus Norrisii, *Sby.*
193. Ziziphinus annulatus, *Mart.*
194. Ziziphinus doliarius, *Chemn.*
195. Ziziphinus filosus, *Wood.*
196. Livona picoides, *Gld.*
197. Osilinus gallina, *Fbs.*
198. Osilinus
199. Omphalius aureotinctus, *Fbs.*
200. Omphalius brunneus, *A. Ad.*
201. Omphalius euryomphalus, *J.*
202. Omphalius fuscescens, *Phil.*
203. Omphalius mæstus, *Jonas.*
204. ?Omphalius marcidus, *Gld.*
205. Omphalius marginatus, *Nutt.*
206. Omphalius Pfeifferi, *Phil.*
207. Margarita callostoma, *A. Ad.*
208. Margarita pupilla, *Gld.*
209. Margarita
210. Margarita
211. Margarita
212. Margarita

PECTINIBRANCHIATA.
Calyptræidæ.

213. Crucibulum spinosum, *Sby.*
214. Galerus fastigiatus, *Gld.*
215. Crepidula aculeata, *Linn.*
216. Crepidula adunca, *Sby.*
217. Crepidula explanata, *Gld.*
218. Crepidula incurva, *Brod.*

(a)

4

219. Crepidula lingulata, *Gld.*
220. Crepidula nummaria, *Gld.*
221. Crepidula rugosa, *Nutt.*
222. Hipponyx antiquatus, *Linn.*
223. Hipponyx barbatus, *Sby.*
224. Hipponyx Grayanus, *Mke.*

Vermetidæ.

225. Aletus squamigerus, *Cpr.*
226. Spiroglyphus
227. Spiroglyphus

Turritellidæ.

228. Mesalia
229. Mesalia

Cerithiadæ.

230. Bittium filosum, *Gld.*
231. Bittium
232. Bittium
233. Cerithidea albonodosa, *Cpr.*
234. Cérithidea pullata, *Gld.*
235. Cerithidea sacrata, *Gld.*

Litorinidæ.

236. Litorina planaxis, *Phil.*
237. Litorina plena, *Gld.*
238. Litorina scutellata, *Gld.*
239. Litorina sitchana, *Phil.*
240. Lacuna carinata, *Gld.*
241. Lacuna unifasciata, *Cpr.*

Ovulidæ.

242. Radius variabilis, *Sby.*

Cypræidæ.

243. Luponia albuginosa, *Gray.*
244. Luponia spadicea, *Swains.*
245. Trivia californica, *Gray.*
246. Erato leucophæa, *Gld.*

Cancellariadæ.

247. Trichotropis cancellata, *Hds.*

Pleurotomidæ.

248. Drillia
249. Daphnella
250. Mangelia
251. Mangelia
252. Bela fidicula, *Gld.*
253. Bela

Conidæ.

254. Conus ravus, *Gld.*

Pyramidellidæ.

255. Odostomia gravida, *Gld.*
256. Odostomia
257. Parthenia
258. Chemnitzia [chocolata].
259. Chemnitzia tenuicula, *Gld.*
260. Chemnitzia torquata, *Gld.*

Eulimidæ.

261. Eulima

Scalariadæ.

262. Scalaria australis, *Phil.*
263. Scalaria [*like* ochotensis].
264. Scalaria

Naticidæ.

265. Natica ?clausa, *Brod. & Sby.*
266. Natica impervia, *Phil.*
267. Lunatia algida, *Gld.*
268. Lunatia caurina, *Gld.*
269. Lunatia Lewisii, *Gld.*
270. Neverita Recluziana, *Rve.*
271. Polinices perspicua, *Recl.*

Tritonidæ.

272. Argobuccinum oregonense, *Redf*

Ranellidæ.

273. Ranella californica, *Hds.*
274. Ranella triquetra, *Rve.*

Mitrinæ.

275. Mitra maura, *Nutt.*

Marginellidæ.

276. Marginella Jewettii, *Cpr.*

Olividæ.

277. Olivella biplicata, *Sby.*
278. Olivella rufofasciata, *Rve.*
279. Olivella

Purpuridæ.

280. Purpura decemcostata, *Midd.*
281. Purpura emarginata, *Desh.*
282. Purpura lactuca, *Esch.*
283. Purpura ostrina, *Gld.*
284. Monoceros engonatum, *Conr.*
285. Monoceros lapilloides, *Conr.*
286. Nitidella Gouldii, *Cpr.*
287. Nitidella
288. Truncaria
289. Cerastoma Belcheri, *Hds.*
290. Cerastoma foliatum, *Esch.*

Buccinidæ.

291. Columbella californiana, *Gask*
292. Columbella carinata, *Hds.*
293. Columbella gausapata, *Gld.*
294. Columbella sta-barbarensis, *C.*
295. Buccinum corrugatum, *Rve.*
296. Nassa fossata, *Gld.*
297. Nassa mendica, *Gld.*

Muricidæ.

298. Chrysodomus antiquus, *Linn.*
299. Chrysodomus Middendorffii,
300. Chrysodomus [*Cooper.*
301. Chrysodomus sitchana, *Midd.*
302. Trophon cancellinum, *Phil.*
303. Trophon corrugatum, *Rve.*
304. Trophon orpheus, *Gld.*
305. Pteronotus festivus, *Hds.*

(a)

CHECK LIST

OF THE

SHELLS OF NORTH AMERICA.

WEST COAST:
MEXICAN AND PANAMIC PROVINCE.

BY

P. P. CARPENTER.

THE West Tropical fauna of America is known to extend from Guaymas in the Gulf of California, to the shores of Ecuador and Peru; and includes the Galapagos Islands. This list contains the Panama Shells of Prof. C. B. Adams; the Mazatlan Shells of the British Museum Catalogue; the species from various sources enumerated in the "Report on the Present State of our Knowledge of the Molluska of the West Coast of N. America,"—British Association, 1856, pp. 289 *et seq.;* and a few since discovered. The synonyms, stragglers from other faunas, and the insular and South American species are omitted. Being prepared simply for the interchange of named specimens, it should not be cited as an authority.

BRYOZOA.
Membraniporidæ.
1. **Membranipora denticulata,** *B.*
2. **Membranipora gothica,** *Ryl.*
3. **Lepralia adpressa,** *Busk.*
4. **Lepralia atrofusca,** *Ryl.*
5. **Lepralia hippocrepis,** *Busk.*
6. **Lepralia humilis,** *Busk.*
7. **Lepralia marginipora,** *Reuss.*
8. **Lepralia mazatlanica,** *Busk.*
9. **Lepralia rostrata,** *Busk.*
10. **Lepralia trispinosa,** *Johnst.*
Celleporidæ.
11. **Cellepora cyclostoma,** *Busk.*
12. **Cellepora papillæformis,** *Busk.*
Discoporidæ.
13. **Defrancia intricata,** *Busk.*

PALLIOBRANCHIATA.
14. **Discina Cumingii,** *Brod.*

LAMELLIBRANCHIATA.
Pholadidæ.
15. **Pholas cornea.**
16. **Pholas crucigera,** *Sby.*
17. **Pholadidea curta,** *Sby.*
18. **Pholadidea melanura,** *Sby.*
19. **Pholadidea tubifera,** *Sby.*
20. **Parapholas acuminata,** *Sby.*
21. **Parapholas calva,** *Gray.*
22. **Martesia intercalata,** *Cpr.*
23. **Martesia xylophaga,** *Val.*
Gastrochænidæ.
24. **Gastrochæna ovata,** *Sby.*
25. **Gastrochæna truncata,** *Sby.*
Saxicavidæ.
26. **Saxicava ?arctica,** *Linn.*
Corbulidæ.
27. **Sphænia fragilis,** *Cpr.*
28. **Potamomya æqualis,** *C. B. Ad.*
29. **Potamomya inflata,** *C. B. Ad.*

30. Potamomya trigonalis, *C. B. A.*
31. Corbula bicarinata, *Sby.*
32. Corbula biradiata, *Sby.*
33. Corbula Boivinei.
34. Corbula fragilis, *Hds.*
35. Corbula marmorata, *Hds.*
36. Corbula nasuta, *Sby.*
37. Corbula nuciformis, *Sby.*
38. Corbula obesa, *Hds.*
39. Corbula ovulata, *Sby.*
40. Corbula pustulosa, *Cpr.*
41. Corbula radiata.
42. Corbula rubra, *C. B. Ad.*
43. Corbula speciosa, *Hds.*
44. Corbula tenuis, *Sby.*
45. Corbula ventricosa, *Rve.*

Anatinidœ.

46. Thracia squamosa, *Cpr.*
47. Tyleria fragilis, *H. & A. Ad.*
48. Lyonsia diaphana, *Cpr.*
49. Lyonsia picta, *Sby.*
50. Periploma alta, *C. B. Ad.*
51. Periploma excurvata, *Cpr.*
52. Periploma Leana, *Conr.*
53. Periploma papyracea, *Cpr.*
54. Periploma planiuscula, *Sby.*
55. Neæra costata, *Hds.*
56. Neæra didyma, *Hds.*
57. Pandora brevifrons.
58. Pandora claviculata, *Cpr.*
59. Pandora cornuta, *C. B. Ad.*

Solenidœ.

60. Solen rudis, *C. B. Ad.*

Solecurtidœ.

61. Solecurtus affinis, *C. B. Ad.*
62. Solecurtus politus, *Cpr.*
63. Solecurtus violascens, *Cpr.*
64. Sanguinolaria miniata, *Gld.*
65. Sanguinolaria tellinoides, *Ad.*
66. Psammobia Kindermanni, *Phil.*
67. Tellina brevirostris, *Desh.*
68. Tellina Broderipii, *Desh.*
69. Tellina cognata, *C. B. Ad.*
70. Tellina columbiensis, *Hanl.*
71. Tellina crystallina, *Chemn.*
72. Tellina Cumingii, *Hanl.*
73. Tellina delicatula, *Desh.*
74. Tellina denticulata, *Desh.*
75. Tellina Deshayesii, *Cpr.*
76. Tellina donacilla, *Cpr.*
77. Tellina eburnea, *Hanl.*
78. Tellina fausta, *Donov.*
79. Tellina felix, *Hanl.*
80. Tellina gemma, *Gld.*
81. Tellina hiberna, *Hanl.*

82. Tellina insculpta, *Hanl.*
83. Tellina laceridens, *Hanl.*
84. Tellina lamellata, *Cpr.*
85. Tellina panamensis.
86. Tellina princeps, *Hanl.*
87. Tellina prora, *Hanl.*
88. Tellina puella, *C. B. Ad.*
89. Tellina punicea, *Born.*
90. Tellina pura, *Gld.*
91. Tellina regia, *Hanl.*
92. Tellina regularis, *Cpr.*
93. Tellina rhodora, *Hanl*
94. Tellina rubescens, *Hanl.*
95. Tellina rufescens, *Chemn.*
96. Tellina siliqua, *C. B. Ad.*
97. Tellina straminea, *Desh.*
98. Tellina virgo, *Hanl.*
99. Macoma aurora, *Hanl.*
100. Macoma concinna, *C. B. Ad.*
101. Macoma Dombeyi, *Hanl.*
102. Macoma elongata, *Hanl.*
103. Macoma gubernaculum, *Hanl*
104. Macoma mazatlanica, *Desh.*
105. Macoma petalum, *Val.*
106. Macoma plebeia, *Hanl.*
107. Macoma tersa, *Gld.*
108. Strigilla carnaria, *Linn.*
109. Strigilla dichotoma, *Phil.*
110. Strigilla disjuncta, *Cpr.*
111. Strigilla ervilia, *Phil.*
112. Strigilla lenticula, *Phil.*
113. Strigilla sincera, *Hanl.*
114. Tellidora Burneti, *Brod. & Sby.*
115. ?Scrobicularia producta, *Cpr.*
116. ?Scrobicularia viriditincta, *C*
117. Semele bicolor, *C. B. Ad.*
118. Semele californica, *A. Ad.*
119. Semele elliptica, *Sby.*
120. Semele flavescens, *Gld.*
121. Semele obliqua, *Wood.*
122. Semele planata.
123. Semele proxima, *C. B. Ad.*
124. Semele pulchra, *Sby.*
125. Semele striosa, *C. B. Ad.*
126. Semele tortuosa, *C. B. Ad.*
127. Semele ventricosa, *C. B. Ad.*
128. Semele ?venusta, *A. Ad.*
129. Cumingia californica, *Conr.*
130. Cumingia lamellosa, *Sby.*
131. Cumingia trigonularis, *Sby.*
132. Cumingia

Donacidœ.

133. Iphigenia altior, *Sby.*
134. Iphigenia lævigata, *Gmel.*
135. Arcopagia vicina, *C. B. Ad.*

8

136. Donax assimilis, *Hanl.*
137. Donax bella, *Desh.*
138. Donax caelatus, *Cpr.*
139. Donax carinatus, *Hanl.*
140. Donax Carpenteri, *II. & A. Ad.*
141. Donax Conradi, *Desh.*
142. Donax culminatus, *Cpr.*
143. Donax gracilis, *Hanl.*
144. Donax navicula, *Hanl.*
145. Donax ovalina, *Desh.*
146. Donax panamensis.
147. Donax punctatostriatus, *Hanl.*
148. Donax transversus, *Sby.*

Mactridæ.

149. Mactra angulata, *Gray.*
150. Mactra angusta, *Desh.*
151. Mactra californica, *Desh.*
152. Mactra exoleta, *Gray.*
153. Mactra fragilis, *Chemn.*
154. Mactra goniata, *Gray.*
155. Mactra laciniata.
156. Mactra pallida.
157. Mactra velata, *Phil..*
158. Raeta elegans, *Sby.*
159. Rangia mendica, *Gld.*

Veneridæ.

160. Clementia gracillima, *Cpr*
161. Trigona argentina, *Sby.*
162. Trigona humilis, *Cpr.*
163. Trigona planulata, *Sby.*
164. Trigona radiata, *Sby.*
165. Dosinia Annæ, *Cpr.*
166. Dosinia Dunkeri, *Phil.*
167. Dosinia ponderosa, *Gray.*
168. Cyclina producta, *Cpr.*
169. Cyclina subquadrata, *Hanl.*
170. Dione aurantia, *Hanl.*
171. Dione brevispinosa, *Sby.*
172. Dione chionæa, *Mke.*
173. Dione circinata, *Born.*
174. Dione concinna, *Sby.*
175. Dione consanguinea, *C. B. Ad.*
176. Dione lupinaria, *Less.*
177. Dione rosea, *Brod. & Sby.*
178. Dione unicolor, *Sby.*
179. Dione vulnerata, *Brod.*
180. Cytherea petichialis, *Lam.*
181. Venus amathusia, *Phil.*
182. Venus californiensis, *Brod.*
183. Venus columbiensis, *Sby.*
184. Venus crenifera, *Sby.*
185. Venus distans, *Phil.*
186. Venus fluctifraga, *Sby.*
187. Venus fuscolineata, *Br. & Sby.*
188. Venus gnidia, *Brod. & Sby.*

189. Venus Kellettii, *Hds.*
190. Venus multicostata, *Sby.*
191. Venus neglecta, *Gray.*
192. Venus ornatissima, *Brod.*
193. Venus pulicaria, *Brod.*
194. Venus reticulata, *Ln.*
195. Venus undatella, *Sby.* [*Sby*
196. Anomalocardia subimbricata,
197. Anomalocardia subrugosa, *S.*
198. Tapes grata, *Say.*
199. Tapes histrionica, *Sby.*
200. Tapes squamosa, *Cpr.*
201. Tapes tenerrima, *Cpr.*

Petricolidæ.

202. Petricola cognata, *C. B. Ad.*
203. Petricola dactylus, *Sby.*
204. Petricola denticulata, *Sby.*
205. Petricola robusta, *Sby.*
206. Petricola ventricosa, *Desh.*
207. Rupellaria exarata, *Cpr.*
208. Rupellaria foliacea, *Desh.*
209. Rupellaria lingua-felis, *Cpr.*
210. Rupellaria paupercula, *Desh.*
211. Naranio scobina, *Cpr.*

Astartidæ.

212. Gouldia pacifica, *C. B. Ad.*
213. Gouldia varians, *Cpr.*
214. Circe margarita, *Cpr.*
215. Circe subtrigona, *Cpr.*
216. Crassatella gibbosa, *Sby.*
217. Trapezium
218. Cardita affinis, *Brod.*
219. Cardita californica, *Desh.*
220. Cardita crassa, *Gray.*
221. Cardita Cuvieri, *Brod.*
222. Cardita laticostata, *Sby.*
223. Cardita radiata, *Brod.*

Chamidæ.

224. Chama Buddiana, *C. B. Ad.*
225. Chama corrugata, *Brod.*
226. Chama echinata, *Brod.*
227. Chama exogyra, *Conr.*
228. Chama frondosa, *Brod.*
229. Chama panamensis, *Rve.*
230. Chama producta, *Brod.*
231. Chama spinosa, *Sby.*

Cardiadæ.

232. Cardium alabastrum, *Cpr.*
233. Cardium Belcheri, *Brod. & Sby.*
234. Cardium biangulatum, *B. & Sby.*
235. Cardium consors, *Brod. & Sby.*
236. Cardium Cumingii, *Brod.*
237. Cardium elatum, *Sby.*
238. Cardium graniferum, *Brod. & S.*
239. Cardium maculosum. *Wood.*

8

(b)

240. Cardium obovale, *Brod. & Sby.*
241. Cardium panamense, *Sby.*
242. Cardium procerum, *Sby.*
243. Cardium rotundatum, *Cpr.*
244. Cardium senticosum, *Sby.*

Lucinidæ.

245. Codakia punctata, *Linn.*
246. Codakia tigerina, *Linn.*
247. Lucina annulata, *Rve.*
248. Lucina artemidis, *Cpr.*
249. Lucina eburnea, *Rve.*
250. Lucina excavata, *Cpr.*
251. Lucina fenestrata.
252. Lucina mazatlanica, *Cpr.*
253. Lucina muricata, *Chemn.*
254. Lucina pectinata, *Cpr.*
255. Lucina prolongata, *Cpr.*

Diplodontidæ.

256. Diplodonta calculus, *Rve.*
257. Diplodonta obliqua, *Phil.*
258. Diplodonta semiaspera, *Phil.*
259. Diplodonta subquadrata, *Cpr.*
260. Felania cornea, *Rve.*
261. Felania serricata, *Rve.*
262. Felania tellinoides, *Rve.*

Kelliadæ.

263. Kellia suborbicularis, *Mont.*
264. Lasea oblonga, *Cpr.*
265. Lasea ?rubra, *Mont.*
266. Lasea trigonalis, *Cpr.*
267. Lepton clementinum, *Cpr.*
268. Lepton dionæum, *Cpr.*
269. Lepton obtusum, *Cpr.*
270. Lepton umbonatum, *Cpr.*
271. Pythina sublævis, *Cpr.*
272. Montacuta chalcedonica, *Cpr.*
273. Montacuta elliptica, *Cpr.*
274. Montacuta subquadrata, *Cpr.*
275. Scintilla Cumingii, *Desh.*
276. [Cycladella papyracea.]

Mytilidæ.

277. Mytilus multiformis, *Cpr.*
278. Mytilus palliopunctatus, *Dkr.*
279. Septifer Cumingianus, *Dkr.*
280. Modiola braziliensis, *Chemn.*
281. Modiola capax, *Conr.*
282. Modiola mutabilis, *Cpr.*
283. Crenella coarctata, *Dkr.*
284. Lithophagus aristatus, *Sol.*
285. Lithophagus attenuatus, *Desh.*
286. Lithophagus calyculatus, *Cpr.*
287. Lithophagus cinnamomeus, *L.*
288. Lithophagus plumula, *Hank.*
289. Leiosolenus spatiosus, *Cpr.*

Arcadæ.

290. Arca cardiiformis, *Sby.*
291. Arca concinna.
292. Arca formosa, *Sby.*
293. Arca grandis, *Brod. & Sby.*
294. Arca multicostata, *Sby.*
295. Arca tuberculosa, *Sby.*
296. Scapharca bifrons, *Cpr.*
297. Scapharca emarginata, *Sby.*
298. Scapharca labiata, *Sby.*
299. Scapharca nux, *Sby.*
300. Noetia reversa, *Gray.*
301. Argina brevifrons, *Sby.*
302. Byssoarca alternata, *Sby.*
303. Byssoarca aviculoides, *Rve.*
304. Byssoarca gradata, *Brod. & Sby*
305. Byssoarca illota, *Sby.*
306. Byssoarca mutabilis, *Sby.*
307. Byssoarca pacifica, *Sby.*
308. Byssoarca Reeviana, *D'Orb.*
309. Byssoarca solida, *Sby.*
310. Byssoarca vespertilio, *Cpr.*
311. Axinæa bicolor, *Rve.*
312. Axinæa gigantea, *Rve.*
313. Axinæa inæqualis, *Sby.*
314. Axinæa maculata, *Brod.*
315. Axinæa multicostata, *Say.*
316. Axinæa parcipicta.
317. Axinæa pectenoides.
318. Nucinella

Nuculidæ.

319. Nucula exigua, *Sby.*
320. Leda costellata, *Sby.*
321. Leda crispa, *Hds.*
322. Leda elenensis, *Sby.*
323. Leda excavata, *Hds.*
324. Leda gibbosa, *Sby.*
325. Leda lyrata, *Hds*
326. Leda polita, *Sby.*

Aviculidæ.

327. Pinna lanceolata, *Sby.*
328. Pinna maura, *Sby.*
329. Pinna rugosa, *Sby.*
330. Pinna tuberculosa, *Sby.*
331. Avicula sterna, *Gld.*
332. Margaritiphora fimbriata, *Dkr*
333. Isognomon Chemnitzianus,
334. Isognomon janus, *Cpr.* [*D'Orb.*

Pectenidæ.

335. Pecten circularis, *Sby.*
336. Pecten fasciculatus, *Hds.*
337. Pecten nodosus, *Ln.*
338. Pecten subnodosus, *Sby.*
339. Pecten tumbezensis, *D'Orb.*
340. Pecten ventricosus, *Sby*

341. Janira dentata, *Sby.*
342. Janira sericea, *Hds.*
343. Lima angulata, *Sby.*
344. Lima arcuata, *Sby.*
345. Lima pacifica, *D'Orb.*
346. Lima tetrica, *Gld.*
 Spondylidæ.
347. Spondylus calcifer, *Cpr.*
348. Spondylus dubius.
349. Spondylus limbatus, *Sby.*
350. Spondylus princeps, *Brod.*
351. Spondylus radula, *Rve.*
352. Plicatula penicillata, *Cpr.*
 Ostreadæ.
353. Ostrea columbiensis, *Hanl.*
354. Ostrea conchaphila, *Cpr.*
355. Ostrea Cumingiana, *Dkr.*
356. Ostrea iridescens, *Gray.*
357. Ostrea palmula, *Cpr.*
358. Ostrea ?Virginica, *Gmel.*
 Anomiadæ.
359. Placunanomia claviculata, *C.*
360. Placunanomia Cumingii, *Brod.*
361. Placunanomia foliata, *Brod.*
362. Placunanomia pernoides, *Gray.*
363. Anomia fidenas, *Gray.*
364. Anomia lampe, *Gray.*

 GASTEROPODA
 OPISTHOBRANCHIATA.
 Pleurobranchidæ.
365. Umbrella ovalis, *Cpr.*
 Philinidæ.
366. Smaragdinella thecaphora, *C.*
 Bullidæ.
367. Bulla Adamsi, *Mke.*
368. Bulla exarata, *Cpr.*
369. Bulla nebulosa, *Gld.*
370. Bulla panamensis, *Phil.*
371. Bulla Quoyii, *Gray.*
372. Haminea cymbiformis, *Cpr.*
373. Haminea vesicula, *Gld.*
 Cylichnidæ.
374. Cylichna luticola, *C. B. Ad.*
375. Tornatina carinata, *Cpr.*
376. Tornatina infrequens, *C. B. Ad.*

 GASTEROPODA
 PULMONATA.
 Auriculidæ.
377. Melampus acutus, *D'Orb.*
378. Melampus Bridgesii, *Cpr.*
379. Melampus concinnus, *C. B. Ad.*
380. Melampus infrequens, *C.B.Ad.*
381. Melampus olivaceus, *Cpr.*

382. Melampus panamensis, *C. B. A.*
383. Melampus stagnalis, *D'Orb.*
384. Melampus tabogensis, *C. B. A.*
385. Melampus trilineatus, *C.B. Ad.*
386. Pedipes angulata, *C. B. Ad.*
 Siphonariadæ.
387. Siphonaria æquilirata, *Cpr.*
388. Siphonaria costata, *Sby.*
389. Siphonaria gigas, *Sby.*
390. Siphonaria lecanium, *Phil.*
391. Siphonaria maura, *Sby*
392. Siphonaria pica, *Sby.*

 GASTEROPODA
 PROSOBRANCHIATA.
 HETEROPODA.
 Ianthinidæ.
393. Ianthina decollata, *Cpr.*
394. Ianthina striulata, *Cpr.*
395. Recluzia Rollandiana, *Phil.*

 CIRRIBRANCHIATA.
 Dentaliadæ.
396. Dentalium corrugatum, *Cpr.*
397. Dentalium hyalinum, *Phil.*
398. Dentalium liratum, *Cpr.*
399. Dentalium pretiosum, *Sby.*
400. Dentalium tessaragonum.

 SCUTIBRANCHIATA.
 Chitonidæ.
401. Lophyrus albolineatus, *B. & S.*
402. Lophyrus articulatus, *B. & Sby.*
403. Lophyrus dispar, *Sby.*
404. Lophyrus lævigatus, *Sby.*
405. Lophyrus Stokesii, *Brod.*
406. Lophyrus striatosquamosus, *C.*
407. Callochiton pulchellus, *Gray.*
408. Lepidopleurus Beanii, *Cpr.*
409. Lepidopleurus bullatus, *Cpr.*
410. Lepidopleurus clathratus, *Cpr.*
411. Lepidopleurus magdalensis, *H.*
412. Lepidopleurus M'Andreæ, *C.*
413. Lepidopleurus sanguineus, *R.*
414. Lepidochiton proprius, *Rve.*
415. Tonicia crenulata, *Brod.*
416. Tonicia Forbesii, *Cpr.*
417. Tonicia lineata, *Wood.*
418. [Chiton] clathratus, *Rve.*
419. Chiton columbiensis, *Sby.*
420. [Chiton] Elenensis, *Sby.*
421. Chiton flavescens, *Cpr.*
422. Chiton luridus, *Sby.*
423. Chiton scabricula, *Sby.*
424. [Chiton] setosus, *Sby.*
425. Mopalia Hindsii, *Sby.*

426. Acanthochites arragonites, *C.*
427. Plaxiphora retusa, *Sby.*
Patellidæ.
428. Patella discors, *Phil.*
429. Patella mexicana, *Brod. & Sby.*
430. Patella pediculus, *Phil.*
431. Patella stipulata, *Rve.*
432. Nacella
Acmæidæ.
433. Acmæa fascicularis, *Mke.*
434. Acmæa livescens, *Rve.*
435. Acmæa mesoleuca, *Mke.*
436. Acmæa mitella, *Mke.*
437. Acmæa scabra, *Nutt.*
438. Acmæa vespertina, *Rve.*
439. Scutellina navicelloides, *Cpr.*
Gadiniadæ.
440. Gadinia pentegoniostoma, *Sby.*
Fissurellidæ.
441. Fissurella alba, *Cpr.*
442. Fissurella crenifera, *Sby.*
443. Fissurella macrotrema, *Sby.*
444. Fissurella mexicana, *Sby.*
445. Fissurella microtrema, *Sby.*
446. Fissurella mus, *Rve.*
447. Fissurella nigrocincta, *Cpr.*
448. Fissurella nigropunctata, *Sby.*
449. Fissurella ostrina, *Rve.*
450. Fissurella rugosa, *Sby.*
451. Fissurella spongiosa, *Cpr.*
452. Fissurella virescens, *Sby.*
453. Glyphis alta, *C. B. Ad.*
454. Glyphis gibberula, *Lam.*
455. Glyphis inæqualis, *Sby.*
456. Glyphis panamensis, *Sby.*
457. Fissurellidæa æqualis, *Sby.*
458. Rimula mazatlanica, *Cpr.*
Trochidæ.
459. Phasianella compta, *Gld.*
460. Phasianella perforata, *Phil.*
461. Callopoma fluctuosum, *Mawe.*
462. Callopoma saxosum, *Wood.*
463. Collonia phasianella, *C. B. Ad.*
464. Turbo rutilus, *C. B. Ad.*
465. Turbo squamigera, *Rve.*
466. Uvanilla inermis, *Gmel.*
467. Uvanilla olivacea, *Mawe.*
468. Uvanilla unguis, *Mawe.*
469. Ziziphinus Leanus, *C. B. Ad.*
470. Ziziphinus lima, *Phil.*
471. Ziziphinus M'Andreæ, *Cpr.*
472. Ziziphinus panamensis, *Phil.*
473. Ziziphinus versicolor, *Mke.*
474. Tegula pellis-serpentis, *Wood.*

475. Gibbula coronulata, *C. B. Ad.*
476. Omphalius globulus, *Cpr.*
477. Omphalius ligulatus, *Mke.*
478. Omphalius rugosus, *A. Ad.*
479. Omphalius viridulus, *Gmel.*
480. Polydonta dentata, *A. Ad.*
481. Vitrinella annulata, *Cpr.*
482. Vitrinella bifilata, *Cpr.*
483. Vitrinella bifrontia, *Cpr.*
484. Vitrinella carinulata, *Cpr.*
485. Vitrinella cincta, *Cpr.*
486. Vitrinella concinna, *C. B. Ad.*
487. Vitrinella coronata, *Cpr.*
488. Vitrinella decussata, *Cpr.*
489. Vitrinella exigua, *C. B. Ad.*
490. Vitrinella janus, *C. B. Ad.*
491. Vitrinella lirulata, *Cpr.*
492. Vitrinella modesta, *C. B. Ad.*
493. Vitrinella monilifera, *Cpr.*
494. Vitrinella monilis, *Cpr.*
495. Vitrinella orbis, *Cpr.*
496. Vitrinella panamensis, *C. B. A.*
497. Vitrinella parva, *C. B. Ad.*
498. Vitrinella perparva, *C. B. Ad.*
499. Vitrinella planospirata, *Cpr.*
500. Vitrinella regularis, *C. B. Ad.*
501. Vitrinella seminuda, *C. B. Ad.*
502. Vitrinella subquadrata, *Cpr.*
503. Vitrinella tricarinata, *C. B. Ad.*
504. Ethalia amplectans, *Cpr.*
505. Ethalia carinata, *Cpr.*
506. Ethalia lirulata, *Cpr.*
507. Ethalia naticoides, *Cpr.*
508. Ethalia pallidula, *Cpr.*
509. Ethalia pyricallosa, *Cpr*
510. Ethalia valvatoides, *C. B. Ad.*
511. Teinostoma amplectans, *Cpr.*
512. Teinostoma minutum, *C. B. Ad.*
513. Teinostoma substriatum, *Cpr.*
514. Globulus sulcatus, *Cpr.*
515. Globulus tumens, *Cpr.*
516. Adeorbis scaber, *Phil.*
Neritidæ.
517. Nerita Bernhardi, *Recl.*
518. Nerita scabricosta, *Lam.*
519. Neritina californica, *Rve.*
520. Neritina cassiculum, *Sby.*
521. Neritina globosa, *Brod.*
522. Neritina guayaquilensis, *Sby.*
523. Neritina intermedia, *Sby.*
524. Neritina latissima, *Brod.*
525. Neritina Listeri, *Pfr.*
526. Neritina Michaudi, *Récl.*
527. Neritina picta, *Sby.*
528. Neritina pulchra, *Wood.*

PECTINIBRANCHIATA.
ROSTRIFERA.
Naricidœ.
529. Narica cryptophila, Cpr.
Calyptrœidœ.
530. Crucibulum imbricatum, Sby.
531. Crucibulum Jewettii, Cpr.
532. Crucibulum radiatum, Brod.
533. Crucibulum serratum.
534. Crucibulum spinosum, Sby.
535. Crucibulum umbrella, Desh.
536. Calyptræa cepacea, Brod.
537. Calyptræa corrugata, Brod.
538. Calyptræa planulata, Brod.
539. Galerus conicus, Brod.
540. Galerus mamillaris, Brod.
541. Galerus sordidus, Brod.
542. Galerus subreflexus, Cpr.
543. Galerus unguis, Brod.
544. Trochita spirata, Forbes.
545. Trochita ventricosa, Cpr.
546. Crepidula aculeata, Gmel.
547. Crepidula adunca, Sby.
548. Crepidula arenata, Brod.
549. Crepidula dorsata, Brod.
550. Crepidula excavata, Brod.
551. Crepidula incurva, Brod.
552. Crepidula marginalis, Brod.
553. Crepidula nivea, C. B. Ad.
554. Crepidula onyx, Sby.
555. Crepidula unguiformis, Lam.
Capulidœ.
556. Hipponyx antiquatus, Linn.
557. Hipponyx barbatus, Sby.
558. Hipponyx Grayanus, Mke.
559. Hipponyx mitrula, Sby.
560. Hipponyx planatus, Cpr.
561. Hipponyx serratus, Cpr.
562. Capulus
Vermetidœ.
563. Aletes centiquadrus, Val.
564. Aletes margaritarum, Val.
565. Vermetus eburneus, Rve.
566. Vermetus Hindsii, Gray.
567. Bivonia albida, Cpr.
568. Bivonia contorta, Cpr.
569. Petaloconchus macrophragma, Cpr.
Cœcidœ.
570. Cæcum abnormale, Cpr.
571. Cæcum clathratum, Cpr.
572. Cæcum corrugulatum, Cpr.
573. Cæcum dextroversum, Cpr.
574. Cæcum elongatum, Cpr.
575. Cæcum farcimen, Cpr.

576. Cæcum firmatum, C. B. Ad.
577. Cæcum glabriforme, Cpr.
578. Cæcum heptagonum, Cpr.
579. Cæcum insculptum, Cpr.
580. Cæcum læve, C. B. Ad.
581. Cæcum laqueatum, C. B. Ad
582. Cæcum liratocinctum, Cpr
583. Cæcum obtusum, Cpr.
584. Cæcum quadratum, Cpr.
585. Cæcum reversum, Cpr.
586. Cæcum subimpressum, Cpr.
587. Cæcum subspirale, Cpr.
588. Cæcum teres, Cpr.
589. Cæcum undatum, Cpr.
Turritellidœ.
590. Turritella fascialis, Rve.
591. Turritella goniostoma, Val.
592. Turritella nodulosa, King.
593. Turritella rubescens, Rve.
594. Turritella tigrina, Kien.
Cerithiadœ.
595. Cerithium alboliratum, Cpr.
596. Cerithium famelicum, C. B. Ad.
597. Cerithium interruptum, Mke.
598. Cerithium irroratum, C. B. Ad.
599. Cerithium maculosum, Kien.
600. Cerithium musicum, Val.
601. Cerithium pacificum, Sby.
602. Cerithium stercusmuscarum, V.
603. Cerithium uncinatum, Gmel.
604. Vertagus fragraria, Val.
605. Vertagus gemmatus, Hds.
606. Cerithidea mazatlanica, Cpr.
607. Cerithidea Montagnei, D'Orb.
608. Cerithidea pulchra, C. B. Ad.
609. Cerithidea varicosa, Sby.
Truncatellidœ.
610. Truncatella Bairdiana, C.B.Ad.
Melaniadœ.
611. Melania Gouldii, H. & A. Ad.
612. Pyrgula quadricostata, Cpr.
Ampullaridœ.
613. Ampullaria Cumingii, King.
614. Ampullaria malleata.
Litorinidœ.
615. Litorina aberrans, Phil.
616. Litorina aspera, Phil.
617. Litorina conspersa, Phil.
618. Litorina coronata, Lam.
619. Litorina fasciata, Gray.
620. Litorina Philippii, Cpr.
621. Litorina pulchra, Phil.
622. Litorina varia, Sby.
623. Modulus catenulatus, Phil.
624. Modulus disculus, Phil.

625. Fossarus abjectus, *C. B. Ad.*
626. Fossarus angiostoma, *C. B. Ad.*
627. Fossarus angulatus, *Cpr.*
628. Fossarus excavatus, *C. B. Ad.*
629. Fossarus foveatus, *C. B. Ad.*
630. Fossarus megasoma, *C. B. Ad.*
631. Fossarus tuberosus, *Cpr.*
632. Isapis maculosa, *Cpr.*
633. Isapis ovoidea, *Gld.*

Rissoidæ.

634. Rissoina clandestina, *C. B. Ad.*
635. Rissoina firmata, *C. B. Ad.*
636. Rissoina fortis, *C. B. Ad.*
637. Rissoina infrequens, *C. B. Ad.*
638. Rissoina janus, *C. B. Ad.*
639. Rissoina stricta, *Mke.*
640. Rissoina Woodwardii, *Cpr.*
641. Barleeia lirata, *Cpr.*
642. Alvania effusa, *Cpr.*
643. Alvania excurvata, *Cpr.*
644. Alvania tumida, *Cpr.*
645. ?Cingula dubiosa, *C. B. Ad.*
646. Cingula paupercula, *C. B. Ad.*
647. Cingula saxicola, *C. B. Ad.*
648. Hydrobia ?ulvæ, *Penn.*

Jeffreysiadæ.

649. Jeffreysia Alderi, *Cpr.*
650. Jeffreysia bifasciata, *Cpr.*
651. Jeffreysia tumens, *Cpr.*

Planaxidæ.

652. Alaba alabastrites, *Cpr.*
653. Alaba conica, *Cpr.*
654. Alaba laguncula, *Cpr.*
655. Alaba mutans, *Cpr.*
656. Alaba scalata, *Cpr.*
657. Alaba supralirata, *Cpr.*
658. Alaba terebralis, *Cpr.*
659. Alaba violacea, *Cpr.*
660. Planaxis nigritella, *Forbes.*
661. Planaxis planicostata, *Sby.*

Ovulidæ.

662. Radius æqualis.
663. Radius avena, *Sby.*
664. Radius inflexus, *Sby.*
665. Radius variabilis, *C. B. Ad.*
666. Ovula emarginata, *Sby.*

Cypræidæ.

667. Cypræa exanthema, *Linn.*
668. Aricia arabicula, *Lam.*
669. Aricia punctulata, *Gray.*
670. Trivia pacifica, *Gray.*
671. Trivia pulla, *Gask.*
672. Trivia pustulata, *Lam.*
673. Trivia radians, *Lam.*
674. Trivia rubescens, *Gray.*

675. Trivia sanguinea, *Gray.*
676. Trivia Solandri, *Gray.*
677. Trivia ?suffusa, *Gray.*
678. Erato columbella, *Mke.*
679. Erato Maugeriæ, *Gray.*
680. Erato scabriuscula, *Gray.*

Cancellariadæ.

681. Cancellaria acuminata, *Sby.*
682. Cancellaria affinis, *C. B. Ad.*
683. Cancellaria albida, *Hds.*
684. Cancellaria bifasciata.
685. Cancellaria brevis, *Sby.*
686. Cancellaria buccinoides, *Sby.*
687. Cancellaria bulbulus, *Sby.*
688. Cancellaria bullata, *Sby.*
689. Cancellaria candida, *Sby.*
690. Cancellaria cassidiformis, *Sby*
691. Cancellaria chrysostoma, *Sby.*
692. Cancellaria clavatula, *Sby.*
693. Cancellaria crenata, *Hds.*
694. Cancellaria decussata, *Sby.*
695. Cancellaria elata, *Hds.*
696. Cancellaria gemmulata, *Sby.*
697. Cancellaria goniostoma, *Sby.*
698. Cancellaria indentata, *Sby.*
699. Cancellaria obesa, *Sby.*
700. Cancellaria pulchra, *Sby.*
701. Cancellaria pygmæa, *C. B. Ad*
702. Cancellaria solida, *Sby.*
703. Cancellaria tessellata, *Sby.*
704. Cancellaria uniplicata, *Sby.*
705. Cancellaria urceolata, *Hds.*
706. Cancellaria ventricosa, *Hds.*

Strombidæ.

707. Strombus galeatus, *Wood.*
708. Strombus gracilior, *Sby.*
709. Strombus granulatus, *Swains.*
710. Strombus peruvianus, *Swains.*

TOXIFERA.

Terebridæ.

711. Subula luctuosa, *Hds.*
712. Subula strigata, *Sby.*
713. Subula varicosa, *Hds.*
714. Euryta aciculata, *Hds.*
715. Euryta fulgurata, *Phil.*
716. Terebra lingualis, *Hds.*
717. Terebra ornata, *Gray.*
718. Terebra robusta, *Hds.*
719. Terebra specillata, *Hds.*
720. Terebra uva.
721. Myurella albocincta, *Cpr.*
722. Myurella armillata, *Hds.*
723. Myurella aspera, *Hds.*
724. Myurella elata, *Hds.*

9

725. Myurella Hindsii, *Cpr.*
726. Myurella larvæformis, *Hds.*
727. Myurella rufocinerea, *Cpr.*
728. Myurella subnodosa, *Cpr.*
729. Myurella tuberculosa, *Hds.*
730. Myurella variegata, *Gray.*
    Pleurotomidæ.
731. Pleurotoma arcuata, *Rve.*
732. Pleurotoma bituberculifera.
733. Pleurotoma cedo-nulli, *Rve.*
734. Pleurotoma clavulus, *Sby.*
735. Pleurotoma funiculata, *Val.*
736. Pleurotoma gracillima.
737. Pleurotoma maculosa, *Sby.*
738. Pleurotoma nobilis, *Hds.*
739. Pleurotoma olivacea, *Sby.*
740. Pleurotoma oxytropis, *Sby.*
741. Pleurotoma picta, *Beck.*
742. Pleurotoma pudica, *Hds.*
743. Pleurotoma tuberculifera, *Brod.*
744. Pleurotoma unimaculata, *Sby.*
745. Drillia albonodosa, *Cpr.*
746. Drillia albovallosa, *Cpr.*
747. Drillia aterrima, *Sby.*
748. Drillia bicolor, *Sby.*
749. Drillia cælebs.
750. Drillia cerithoidea, *Cpr.*
751. Drillia collaris, *Sby.*
752. Drillia corrugata, *Sby.*
753. Drillia duplicata, *Sby.*
754. Drillia excentrica, *Sby.*
755. Drillia grandimaculata, *C.B.A.*
756. Drillia granulosa, *Sby.*
757. Drillia Hanleyi, *Cpr.*
758. Drillia impressa, *Hds.*
759. Drillia incrassata, *Sby.*
760. Drillia luctuosa, *Hds.*
761. Drillia militaris, *Hds.*
762. Drillia monilifera, *Cpr.*
763. Drillia nigerrima, *Sby.*
764. Drillia nitida, *Sby.*
765. Drillia obeliscus, *Rve.*
766. Drillia pallida, *Sby.*
767. Drillia pardalis, *Hds.*
768. Drillia punctatostriata.
769. Drillia rudis, *Sby.*
770. Drillia rustica, *Sby.*
771. Drillia striosa, *C. B. Ad.*
772. Drillia unicolor, *Sby.*
773. Drillia zonulata, *Rve.*
774. Clathurella aurea, *Cpr.*
775. Clathurella bella, *Hds.*
776. Clathurella bicanalifera, *Sby.*
777. Clathurella cælata, *Hds.*
778. Clathurella candida, *Hds.*

779. Clathurella cornuta.
780. Clathurella corrugata.
781. Clathurella ericea, *Hds.*
782. Clathurella exigua, *C. B. Ad.*
783. Clathurella gemmulosa, *C.B.A*
784. Clathurella intercalaris.
785. Clathurella merita, *Hds.*
786. Clathurella micans, *Hds.*
787. Clathurella neglecta, *Hds.*
788. Clathurella occata, *Hds.*
789. Clathurella quisqualis, *Hds.*
790. Clathurella rava, *Hds.*
791. Clathurella rigida, *Hds.*
792. Clathurella sculpta, *Hds.*
793. Clathurella serrata.
794. Clathurella variculosa, *Sby.*
795. Daphnella casta, *Hds.*
796. Cithara sinuata.
797. Cithara stromboides, *Rve.*
798. Mangelia acuticostata, *Cpr.*
799. Mangelia concinna, *C. B. Ad.*
800. Mangelia neglecta, *C. B. Ad.*
801. Mangelia sulcosa, *Sby.*
    Conidæ.
802. Conus archon, *Brod.*
803. Conus arcuatus, *Brod. & Sby.*
804. Conus brunneus, *Wood*
805. Conus cinctus.
806. Conus concinnus, *Brod*
807. Conus ferrugatus.
808. Conus gladiator, *Brod.*
809. Conus lineolatus.
810. Conus Lorenzianus, *Chemn.*
811. Conus mahogani, *Rve.*
812. Conus nux, *Brod.*
813. Conus orion, *Brod.*
814. Conus patricius, *Hds.*
815. Conus princeps, *Linn.*
816. Conus puncticulatus, *Hwass.*
817. Conus purpurascens, *Brod.*
818. Conus pusillus, *Chemn.*
819. Conus pyriformis, *Rve.*
820. Conus ravus, *Gld.*
821. Conus regalitatis, *Sby*
822. Conus regularis, *Sby.*
823. Conus scalaris, *Val.*
824. Conus tornatus, *Brod.*
825. Conus vittatus, *Brug.*
826. Conus Ximenes, *Gray.*

    PROBOSCIDIFERA.
    Solariadæ.
827. Solarium granulatum, *Lam.*
828. Solarium quadriceps, *Hds.*
829. Torinia bicanaliculata.

(b)

830. Torinia granosa, *Val.*
831. Torinia variegata, *Lam.*
Pyramidellidæ.
832. Obeliscus clavulus, *A. Ad.*
833. Obeliscus conicus, *C. B. Ad.*
834. Odostomia lamellata, *Cpr.*
835. Odostomia mamillata, *Cpr.*
836. Odostomia sublirulata, *Cpr.*
837. Odostomia subsulcata, *Cpr.*
838. Odostomia tenuis, *Cpr.*
839. Odostomia vallata, *Cpr.*
840. Parthenia armata, *Cpr.*
841. Parthenia exarata, *Cpr.*
842. Parthenia lacunata, *Cpr.*
843. Parthenia quinquecincta, *Cpr.*
844. Parthenia scalariformis, *Cpr.*
845. Parthenia ziziphina, *Cpr.*
846. Chrysallida clathratula, *C.B.A.*
847. Chrysallida clausiliformis, *Cpr.*
848. Chrysallida communis, *C.B.A.*
849. Chrysallida convexa, *Cpr.*
850. Chrysallida effusa, *Cpr.*
851. Chrysallida fasciata, *Cpr.*
852. Chrysallida indentata, *Cpr.*
853. Chrysallida marginata, *C.B.Ad.*
854. Chrysallida nodosa, *Cpr.*
855. Chrysallida oblonga, *Cpr.*
856. Chrysallida ovata, *Cpr.*
857. Chrysallida ovulum, *Cpr.*
858. Chrysallida paupercula, *C.B.A.*
859. Chrysallida photis, *Cpr.*
860. Chrysallida Reigeni, *Cpr.*
861. Chrysallida rotundata, *Cpr.*
862. Chrysallida telescopium, *Cpr.*
863. Chemnitzia aculeus, *C. B. Ad.*
864. Chemnitzia acuminata, *C. B. A.*
865. Chemnitzia C-B-Adamsi, *Cpr.*
866. Chemnitzia affinis, *C. B. Ad.*
867. Chemnitzia flavescens, *Cpr.*
868. Chemnitzia gibbosa, *Cpr.*
869. Chemnitzia gracilior, *C. B. Ad.*
870. Chemnitzia gracillima, *Cpr.*
871. Chemnitzia major, *C. B. Ad.*
872. Chemnitzia muricata, *Cpr.*
873. Chemnitzia panamensis, *C.B.A.*
874. Chemnitzia prolongata, *Cpr.*
875. Chemnitzia similis, *C. B. Ad.*
876. Chemnitzia striosa, *C. B. Ad.*
877. Chemnitzia tenuilirata, *Cpr.*
878. Chemnitzia terebralis, *Cpr.*
879. Chemnitzia turrita, *C. B. Ad.*
880. Chemnitzia undata, *Cpr.*
881. Chemnitzia unifasciata, *Cpr.*
882. Dunkeria cancellata, *Cpr.*
883. Dunkeria intermedia, *Cpr.*

884. Dunkeria paucilirata, *Cpr.*
885. Dunkeria subangulata, *Cpr.*
886. Eulimella obsoleta, *Cpr.*
887. Aclis fusiformis, *Cpr.*
888. Aclis tumens, *Cpr.*
Eulimidæ.
889. Eulima acuta, *A. Ad.*
890. Eulima hastata, *Sby.*
891. Eulima interrupta.
892. Leiostraca distorta, *Phil.*
893. Leiostraca [involuta, *Cpr.*]
894. Leiostraca iota, *C. B. Ad.*
895. Leiostraca linearis, *Cpr.*
896. Leiostraca [producta, *Cpr.*]
897. Leiostraca recta, *C. B. Ad.*
898. Leiostraca retexta, *Cpr.*
899. Leiostraca solitaria, *C. B. Ad.*
Cerithiopsidæ.
900. Cerithiopsis assimilata, *C.B.A.*
901. Cerithiopsis bimarginata, *C.B.A.*
902. Cerithiopsis cerea, *Cpr.*
903. Cerithiopsis convexa, *Cpr.*
904. Cerithiopsis decussata, *Cpr.*
905. Cerithiopsis neglecta, *C. B. A.*
906. Cerithiopsis pupiformis, *Cpr.*
907. Cerithiopsis sorex, *Cpr.*
908. Cerithiopsis tuberculoides, *C.*
909. Cerithiopsis tuberculatus, *C. B. Ad.*
910. Triforis inconspicuus, *C. B. Ad.*
Scalariadæ.
911. Scalaria aciculina, *Hds.*
912. Scalaria Cumingii.
913. Scalaria dianæ, *Hds.*
914. Scalaria hexagona, *Sby.*
915. Scalaria Hindsii
916. Scalaria indistincta, *Sby.*
917. Scalaria mitræformis, *Sby.*
918. Scalaria obtusa.
919. Scalaria raricostata, *Cpr.*
920. Scalaria reflexa, *Cpr.*
921. Scalaria regularis.
922. Scalaria statuminata, *Sby.*
923. Scalaria subnodosa.
924. Scalaria suprastriata, *Cpr.*
925. Scalaria tiara.
926. Scalaria vulpina, *Hds.*
927. Cirsotrema funiculata, *Cpr.*
Naticidæ.
928. Natica bifasciata, *Gray.*
929. Natica excavata, *Cpr.*
930. Natica Haneti, *Récl.*
931. Natica maroccana, *Chemn.*
932. Natica Souleyetiana, *Récl.*
933. Natica zonaria, *Récl.*
934. Lunatia Bonplandi.

935. Lunatia lurida.
936. Lunatia otis, *Brod. & Sby.*
937. Lunatia tenuilirata, *Cpr.*
938. Neverita glauca, *Val.*
939. Polinices intemerata.
940. Polinices panamensis, *Récl.*
941. Polinices salangonensis, *Récl.*
942. Polinices uber, *Val.*
943. Polinices unimaculata, *Rve.*
944. Polinices virginea, *Récl.*
945. Sigaretus debilis, *Gld.*

Lamellariadæ.
946. Lamellaria inflata, *C. B. Ad.*

Ficulidæ.
947. Ficula ventricosa, *Sby.*

Doliadæ.
948. Malea ringens, *Sby.*

Cassidæ.
949. Oniscia tuberculosa, *Rve.*
950. Cassis abbreviata, *Lam.*
951. Cassis coarctata, *Sby.*

Tritonidæ.
952. Triton anomalus, *Hds.*
953. Triton constrictus, *Brod.*
954. Triton crebristriatus.
955. Triton eximius, *Rve.*
956. Triton fusoides, *C. B. Ad.*
957. Triton gibbosus, *Brod.*
958. Triton lignarius, *Brod.*
959. Triton scalariformis, *Brod.*
960. Triton tigrinus, *Brod.*
961. Triton vestitus, *Hds.*
962. Argobuccinum nodosum, *Ch.*
963. Persona ridens, *Rve.*
964. Ranella albifasciata, *Sby.*
965. Ranella anceps, *Lam.*
966. Ranella cælata, *Brod.*
967. Ranella convoluta.
968. Ranella muriciformis, *Brod.*
969. Ranella nana, *Brod.*
970. Ranella nitida, *Brod.*
971. Ranella pectinata, *Hds.*
972. Ranella plicata, *Rve.*
973. Ranella pyramidalis.
974. Ranella triquetra, *Rve.*
975. Ranella tuberculata.

Turbinellidæ.
976. Turbinella cæstus, *Brod.*

Fasciolariadæ.
977. Lathirus armatus.
978. Lathirus californicus.
979. Lathirus castaneus, *Gray.*
980. Lathirus ceratus, *Gray.*
981. Lathirus concentricus, *Rve.*

982. Lathirus nodatus, *Mart.*
983. Lathirus rudis, *Rve.*
984. Lathirus spadiceus, *Rve.*
985. Lathirus tuberculatus, *Brod.*
986. Lathirus tumens.
987. Leucozonia cingulata, *Lam.*

Mitrinæ.
988. Mitra attenuata, *Rve.*
989. Mitra badia, *Rve.*
990. Mitra Belcheri, *Hds.*
991. Mitra funiculata, *Rve.*
992. Mitra Hindsii.
993. Mitra lens, *Wood.*
994. Mitra nucleola, *Lam.*
995. Mitra solitaria, *C. B. Ad.*
996. Mitra sulcata, *Swains.*
997. Strigatella effusa, *Swains.*
998. Strigatella tristis, *Brod.*

Volutidæ.
999. Voluta Cumingii, *Brod.*
1000. Voluta harpa, *Mawe.*
1001. Marginella cærulescens, *Lam.*
1002. Marginella curta, *Sby.*
1003. Marginella cypræola.
1004. Marginella margaritula, *Cpr.*
1005. Marginella minor, *C. B. Ad.*
1006. Marginella polita, *Cpr.*
1007. Marginella sapotilla, *Hds.*
1008. Persicula imbricata, *Hds.*

Olividæ.
1009. Oliva angulata, *Lam.*
1010. Oliva Cumingii, *Rve.*
1011. Oliva Duclosi, *Rve.*
1012. Oliva intertincta, *Cpr.*
1013. Oliva julieta, *Ducl.*
1014. Oliva Melchersi, *Mke.*
1015. Oliva porphyria, *Linn.*
1016. Oliva splendidula, *Sby.*
1017. Oliva venulata, *Lam.*
1018. Olivella anazora, *Ducl.*
1019. Olivella aureocincta, *Cpr.*
1020. Olivella dama, *Mawe.*
1021. Olivella eburnea, *Lam.*
1022. Olivella gracilis, *Gray.*
1023. Olivella inconspicua, *C. B. A.*
1024. Olivella intorta.
1025. Olivella pellucida, *Gray.*
1026. Olivella semistriata, *Gray.*
1027. Olivella tergina, *Ducl.*
1028. Olivella undatella, *Lam.*
1029. Olivella volutella, *Lam.*
1030. Olivella zonalis *Lam.*
1031. Agaronia testacea, *Lam.*
1032. Harpa crenata, *Swains.*
1033. Harpa scriba.

Purpuridæ.

1034. Purpura biserialis, *Blainv.*
1035. Purpura columellaris, *Lam.*
1036. Purpura melo, *Ducl.*
1037. Purpura muricata, *Gray.*
1038. Purpura patula, *Linn.*
1039. Purpura planospira, *Lam.*
1040. Purpura triangularis, *Blainv.*
1041. Purpura triserialis, *Blainv.*
1042. Cuma costata, *Blainv.*
1043. Cuma kiosquiformis, *Ducl.*
1044. Cuma tecta, *Wood.*
1045. Rhizocheilus asper.
1046. Rhizocheilus nux, *Rve.*
1047. Vitularia salebrosa, *King.*
1048. Monoceros brevidentatum, *G.*
1049. Monoceros lugubre, *Sby.*
1050. Monoceros tuberculatum, *Gr.*
1051. Engina alveolata, *Kien.*
1052. Engina carbonaria, *Rve.*
1053. Engina contracta, *Rve.*
1054. Engina crocostoma, *Rve.*
1055. Engina heptagonalis.
1056. Engina jugosa, *C. B. Ad.*
1057. Engina maura.
1058. Engina pyrostoma, *Sby.*
1059. Engina Reeviana, *C. B. Ad.*
1060. Nitidella cribraria, *Lam.*
1061. Nitidella pulchrior, *C. B. Ad.*

Buccinidæ.

1062. Columbella castanea, *Sby.*
1063. Columbella cervinetta, *Cpr.*
1064. Columbella festiva, *Kien.*
1065. Columbella fuscata, *Sby.*
1066. Columbella hæmastoma, *Sby.*
1067. Columbella harpiformis, *Sby.*
1068. Columbella labiosa, *Sby.*
1069. Columbella ligata.
1070. Columbella livida.
1071. Columbella major, *Sby.*
1072. Columbella nasuta.
1073. Columbella pardalis.
1074. Columbella procera.
1075. Columbella strombiformis, *L.*
1076. Metula Hindsii, *II. & A. Ad.*
1077. Truncaria modesta, *Pws.*
1078. ?Buccinum leiocheilus.
1079. ?Buccinum panamense.
1080. Nassa canescens, *C. B. Ad.*
1081. Nassa collaria, *Gld.*
1082. Nassa corpulenta, *C. B. Ad.*
1083. Nassa crebristriata, *Cpr.*
1084. Nassa festiva, *Pws.*
1085. Nassa gemmulosa, *C. B. Ad.*
1086. Nassa glauca, *C. B. Ad.*

1087. Nassa luteostoma, *Brod. & Sby*
1088. Nassa mœsta.
1089. Nassa nodifera, *Pws.*
1090. Nassa pagodus, *C. B. Ad.*
1091. Nassa pallida.
1092. ?Nassa panamensis, *C. B. Ad.*
1093. Nassa scabriuscula, *Pws.*
1094. Nassa striata, *C. B. Ad.*
1095. Nassa tegula, *Rve.*
1096. Nassa versicolor, *C. B. Ad.*
1097. Nassa Wilsoni, *C. B. Ad.*
1098. Phos articulatus, *Hds.*
1099. Phos biplicatus.
1100. Phos crassus, *Hds*
1101. Phos gaudens, *Hds*
1102. Phos turritus, *A. Ad.*
1103. Phos veraguensis, *Hds.*

Pyrulidæ.

1104. Pyrula patula, *Brod. & Sby.*

Muricidæ.

1105. Fusus ambustus.
1106. Fusus apertus, *Cpr.*
1107. Fusus bellus.
1108. Fusus Dupetithouarsii, *Kien.*
1109. Fusus lignarius, *Rve.*
1110. Fusus pallidus, *Brod. & Sby.*
1111. Fusus tumens, *Cpr.*
1112. Trophon Hindsii, *Cpr.*
1113. Anachis albonodosa, *Cpr.*
1114. Anachis atramentaria, *Sby*
1115. Anachis Boivinei, *Kien.*
1116. Anachis conspicua, *C. B. Ad*
1117. Anachis coronata, *Sby.*
1118. Anachis costellata, *Brod. & Sb.*
1119. Anachis diminuta, *C. B. Ad.*
1120. Anachis fluctuata, *Sby.*
1121. Anachis fulva, *Sby.*
1122. Anachis Gaskoinei, *Cpr*
1123. Anachis gracilis, *C. B. Ad.*
1124. Anachis lentiginosa, *Hds.*
1125. Anachis lyrata, *Sby.*
1126. Anachis mœsta, *C. B. Ad.*
1127. Anachis nigricans, *Sby.*
1128. Anachis nigrofusca, *Cpr.*
1129. Anachis nucleolus, *Phil.*
1130. Anachis pallida, *Phil.*
1131. Anachis parva, *Sby.*
1132. Anachis pygmæa, *Sby.*
1133. Anachis rufotincta, *Cpr.*
1134. Anachis rugosa, *Sby.*
1135. Anachis scalarina, *Sby.*
1136. Anachis serrata, *Cpr.*
1137. Anachis tæniata, *Phil.*
1138. Anachis tessellata, *C. B. Ad.*
1139. Anachis varia, *Sby.*

1140. Strombina angularis, *Sby.*
1141. Strombina bicanalifera, *Sby.*
1142. Strombina dorsata, *Sby.*
1143. Strombina elegans, *Sby.*
1144. Strombina fusiformis, *Hds.*
1145. Strombina gibberula, *Sby.*
1146. Strombina maculosa, *Sby.*
1147. Strombina pulcherrima, *Sby.*
1148. Strombina turrita, *Sby.*
1149. Pisania æquilirata, *Cpr.*
1150. Pisania gemmata, *Rve.*
1151. Pisania insignis, *Rve.*
1152. Pisania lugubris, *C. B. Ad.*
1153. Pisania nigrocostata, *Rve.*
1154. Pisania pagodus, *Rve.*
1155. Pisania panamensis, *Phil.*
1156. Pisania pastinaca, *Rve.*
1157. Pisania ringens, *Rve.*
1158. Pisania sanguinolenta, *Ducl.*
1159. Pisania Stimpsoniana, *C.B.A.*
1160. Northia pristis, *Desh.*
1161. Clavella distorta, *Bligh.*
1162. Murex armatus.
1163. Murex erosus, *Brod.*
1164. Murex horridus, *Brod.*

1165. Murex plicatus, *Sby.*
1166. Murex rectirostris, *Sby.*
1167. Murex recurvirostris, *Brod.*
1168. Pteronotus centrifugus, *Hds.*
1169. Phyllonotus bicolor, *Val.*
1170. Phyllonotus brassica, *Lam.*
1171. Phyllonotus imperialis, *Sw.*
1172. Phyllonotus nigritus, *Phil.*
1173. Phyllonotus nitidus, *Brod.*
1174. Phyllonotus oxyacanthus, *Br*
1175. Phyllonotus princeps, *Brod.*
1176. Phyllonotus radix, *Lam.*
1177. Phyllonotus regius, *Swains.*
1178. Muricidea alveata, *Kien.*
1179. Muricidea dubia, *Swains.*
1180. Muricidea fimbriata, *Hds*
1181. Muricidea incisa, *Brod.*
1182. Muricidea lappa, *Brod.*
1183. Muricidea pauxillus, *A. Ad.*
1184. Muricidea radicata, *Hds.*
1185. Muricidea vibex, *Brod.*
1186. Muricidea vittata, *Brod.*
1187. Typhis fimbriatus.
1188. Typhis grandis.
1189. Typhis quadratus, *Hds.*

(*b*)

CHECK LIST

OF THE

SHELLS OF NORTH AMERICA.

EAST COAST:

ARCTIC SEAS TO GEORGIA.

BY

WM. STIMPSON.

THE following catalogue is offered as an exposition of the present state of our knowledge of the molluscous fauna of the eastern coast of North America, from the arctic seas to Georgia, inclusive. It is the result of an attentive search of all *published* accounts relating to the subject, and no species is included that has not been thus announced as an inhabitant of our shores by competent authority ; although others are known to exist there, which have not yet been properly determined. All synonyms have been carefully eliminated. Under the head of "Doubtful Species" we have added a list of the names both of those the existence of which upon our coast is uncertain, and of those which will probably prove identical with species already catalogued.

BRYOZOA.

1. Pedicellina americana, *Leidy.*
2. Bowerbankia gracilis, *Leidy.*
3. Valkeria pustulosa, *Ellis.*
4. Eschara foliacea, *Linn.*
5. Escharina variabilis, *Leidy.*
6. Escharina pediostoma, *Leidy.*
7. Escharina lineata, *Leidy.*
8. Flustra truncata, *Lin.*
9. Flustra solida, *Stm.*
10. Cellularia ternata, *Ellis.*
11. Cellularia densa, *Desor.*
12. Cellularia fastigiata, *Blum.*
13. Cellularia turrita, *Desor.*
14. Membranipora tenuis, *Desor.*
15. Lepralia annulata, *Johnst.*
16. Lepralia sordida, *Stm.*
17. Lepralia rubens, *Stm.*
18. Lepralia crassispina, *Stm.*
19. Lepralia labiata, *Stm.*
20. Hippothoa rugosa, *Stm.*
21. Gemellaria dumosa, *Stm.*
22. Crisia denticulata, *Johnst.*
23. Crisia cribraria, *Stm.*
24. Idmonea pruinosa, *Stm.*
25. Tubulipora divisa, *Stm.*
26. Tubulipora patina, *Johnst.*
27. Tubulipora crates, *Stm.*

TUNICATA.

28. Botryllus stellatus, *Pallas.*
29. Synoicum turgens, *Phipps.*
30. Salpa Caboti, *Desor.*
31. Boltenia clavata, *O. Fabr.*
32. Boltenia rubra, *Stm.*
33. Pera pellucida, *Stm.*
34. Cynthia crystallina, *Möll.*
35. Cynthia pyriformis, *Rathke.*
36. Cynthia subcaerulea, *Stm.*
37. Cynthia partita, *Stm.*

38. Cynthia vittata, *Stm.*
39. Cynthia echinata, *Lin.*
40. Cynthia complanata, *O. Fabr.*
41. Cynthia gutta, *Stm.*
42. Cynthia monocera, *Möll.*
43. Cynthia conchilega, *Müll.*
44. Glandula glutinans, *Möll.*
45. Glandula mollis, *Stm.*
46. Glandula fibrosa, *Stm.*
47. Molgula arenata, *Stm.*
48. Molgula sordida, *Stm.*
49. Molgula producta, *Stm.*
50. Ascidia manhattensis, *DeKay.*
51. Ascidia tenella, *Stm.*
52. Ascidia lurida, *Möll.*
53. Ascidia callosa, *Stm.* [*Sow.*
54. Chelysoma Macleayana, *Br. &*
55. Chelysoma geometrica, *Stm.*
56. Pelonaia arenifera, *Stm.*

PALLIOBRANCHIATA.

57. Lingula pyramidata, *Stm.*
58. Rhynchonella psittacea, *Gm.*
59. Terebratella labradorensis, *Sow.*
60. Waldheimia cranium, *Müll.*
61. Terebratulina septentrionalis, *Couth.*

LAMELLIBRANCHIATA.

62. Anomia ephippium, *Lin.*
63. Anomia aculeata, *Gm.*
64. Ostrea virginiana, *Lister.*
65. Ostrea borealis, *Lam.*
66. Ostrea triangularis, *Holmes.*
67. Ostrea fundata, *Say.*
68. Ostrea equestris, *Say.*
69. Ostrea semicylindrica, *Say.*
70. Plicatula barbadensis, *Petiv.*
71. Lima sulculus, *Leach.*
72. Lima scabra, *Born.*
73. Pecten tenuicostatus, *Migh.*
74. Pecten islandicus, *Ch.*
75. Pecten fuscus, *Gould.*
76. Pecten nodosus, *Lin.*
77. Pecten dislocatus, *Say.*
78. Pecten irradians, *Lam.*
79. Pecten groenlandicus, *Sow.*
80. Axinaea charlestonensis, *Holm.*
81. Arca Holmesii, *Kurtz.*
82. Arca pexata, *Say.*
83. Arca americana, *Gray.*
84. Arca caelata, *Con.*
85. Arca transversa, *Say.*
86. Arca glacialis, *Gray.*
87. Arca lienosa, *Say.*

88. Arca noae, *Lin.*
89. Arca ponderosa, *Say.*
90. Arca incongrua, *Say.*
91. Nucula inflata, *Hanc.*
92. Nucula expansa, *Reeve.*
93. Nucula tenuis, *Mont.*
94. Nucula delphinodonta, *Migh.*
95. Nucula proxima, *Say.*
96. Yoldia pygmaea, *Muenst.*
97. Yoldia arctica, *Gray.*
98. Yoldia sulcifera, *Reeve.*
99. Yoldia siliqua, *Reeve.*
100. Yoldia thraciformis, *Storer.*
101. Yoldia sapotilla, *Gould.*
102. Yoldia limatula, *Say.*
103. Yoldia myalis, *Couth.*
104. Leda buccata, *Möll.*
105. Leda tenuisulcata, *Couth.*
106. Leda minuta, *Müll.*
107. Leda acuta, *Con.*
108. Pinna squamosissima, *Phil.*
109. Pinna carolinensis, *Hanl.*
110. Avicula atlantica, *Lam.*
111. Lithophagus aristatus, *Sol.*
112. Dacrydium vitreum, *Möll.*
113. Crenella glandula, *Tott.*
114. Crenella pectinula, *Gould.*
115. Modiolaria nigra, *Gray.*
116. Modiolaria substriata, *Gray.*
117. Modiolaria laevigata, *Gray.*
118. Modiolaria. discors, *Lin.*
119. Modiolaria corrugata, *Stm.*
120. Modiolaria lateralis, *Say.*
121. Modiola carolinensis, *Con.*
122. Modiola plicatula, *Lam.*
123. Modiola vulgaris, *Fleming.*
124. Modiola americana, *Leach.*
125. Modiola castanea, *Say.*
126. Mytilus edulis, *Lin.*
127. Mytilus cubitus, *Say.*
128. Dreissena leucopheata, *Con.*
129. Chama macrophylla, *Chemn.*
130. Chama arcinella, *Lin.*
131. Cardium elegantulum, *Möll.*
132. Cardium magnum, *Born.*
133. Cardium isocardia, *Lin.*
134. Cardium muricatum, *Lin.*
135. Cardium pinnulatum, *Con.*
136. Cardium islandicum, *Lin.*
137. Liocardium serratum, *Lin*
138. Liocardium Mortoni, *Con.*
139. Serripes groenlandicus, *Ch.*
140. Lucina contracta, *Say.*
141. Lucina crenulata, *Con.*
142. Lucina radians, *Con.*

3

143. Lucina edentula, *Lin.*
144. Lucina filosa, *Stm.*
145. Lucina squamosa, *Lam.*
146. Lucina tigerina, *Lin.*
147. Lucina strigilla, *Stm.*
148. Cryptodon Gouldii, *Phil.*
149. Diplodonta ? punctata, *Say.*
150. Kellia planulata, *Stm.*
151. Turtonia minuta, *O. Fabr.*
152. Montacuta ferruginosa, *Mont.*
153. Montacuta elevata, *Stm.*
154. Lepton lepidum, *Say.*
155. Lepton fabagella, *Con.*
156. Lepton longipes, *Stm.*
157. Cyprina islandica, *Lin.*
158. Astarte Banksii, *Leach.*
159. Astarte striata, *Leach.*
160. Astarte semisulcata, *Leach.*
161. Astarte crebricostata, *Forbes.*
162. Astarte lactea, *Br. & Sow.*
163. Astarte compressa, *Lin.*
164. Astarte portlandica, *Migh.*
165. Astarte quadrans, *Gould.*
166. Astarte castanea, *Say.*
167. Astarte lunulata, *Con.*
168. Cardita borealis, *Con.*
169. Cardita tridentata, *Say.*
170. Cardita floridana, *Con.*
171. Mercenaria violacea, *Schum.*
172. Mercenaria Mortoni, *Con.*
173. Mercenaria notata, *Say.*
174. Gemma Tottenii, *Stm.*
     Venus gemma, Totten.
175. Chione alveata, *Con.*
176. Chione cribraria, *Con.*
177. Chione cancellata, *Lin.*
178. Chione inaequalis, *Say.*
179. Chione trapezoidalis, *Kurtz.*
180. Callista gigantea, *Chemn.*
181. Callista maculata, *Lin.*
182. Callista convexa, *Say.*
183. Dosinia discus, *Reeve.*
184. Tapes fluctuosa, *Gould.*
185. Petricola pholadiformis, *Lam.*
186. Raeta canaliculata, *Say.*
187. Raeta lineata, *Say.*
188. Mactra oblonga, *Say.*
189. Mactra polynyma, *Stm.*
     M. ovalis, Gould.
190. Mactra solidissima, *Chemn.*
191. Mactra similis, *Say.*
192. Mactra lateralis, *Say.*
193. Mactra nucleus, *Con.*
194. Ceronia arctata, *Con.*
195. Ceronia deaurata, *Turt.*
196. Donax fossor, *Say.*
197. Donax variabilis, *Say.*
198. Cumingia tellinoides, *Con.*
199. Semele orbiculata, *Say.*
200. Abra equalis, *Say.*
201. Tellina alternata, *Say.*
202. Tellina polita, *Say.*
203. Tellina tenera, *Say*
204. Tellina tenta, *Say.*
205. Tellina iris, *Say.*
206. Tellina brevifrons, *Say.*
207. Tellina elucens, *Migh.*
208. Tellina decora, *Say.*
209. Tellina lateralis, *Say.*
210. Tellina constricta, *Brug.*
211. Tellina lusoria, *Say.*
212. Strigilla flexuosa, *Say.*
213. Strigilla carnaria, *Lin.*
214. Macoma fusca, *Say.*
215. Macoma sabulosa, *Spengl.*
216. Macoma fragilis, *O. Fabr.*
217. Tellidora lunulata, *Holmes.*
218. Solen ensis, *Lin.*
219. Solen viridis, *Say.*
220. Machaera costata, *Say.*
221. Machaera squama, *Blainv.*
222. Siliquaria gibba, *Spengl.*
223. Siliquaria bidens, *Chemn.*
224. Solenomya velum, *Say.*
225. Solenomya borealis, *Tott.*
226. Mya truncata, *Lin.*
227. Mya arenaria, *Lin.*
228. Corbula contracta, *Say*
229. Neaera pellucida, *Stm.*
230. Cyrtodaria siliqua, *Spengl.*
231. Panopaea norvegica, *Spengl.*
232. Panopaea americana, *Con.*
233. Saxicava distorta, *Say.*
234. Saxicava arctica, *Lin.*
235. Anatina papyracea, *Say.*
236. Cochlodesma Leana, *Con.*
237. Thracia truncata, *Migh.*
238. Thracia myopsis, *Möll.*
239. Thracia Conradi, *Couth.*
240. Lyonsia arenosa, *Möll*
241. Lyonsia hyalina, *Con.*
242. Pandora trilineata, *Say*
243. Pholas costata, *Lin.*
244. Pholas truncata, *Say.*
245. Pholas oblongata, *Say.*
246. Pholas semicostata, *Lea*
247. Pholas crispata, *Lin.*
248. Pholadidea cuneiformis, *Say*
249. Xylotrya palmulata, *Lam.*
250. Teredo dilatata, *Stm.*

GASTEROPODA.

PTEROPODA.

251. Clione limacina, *Phipps*.
252. Heterofusus balea, *Möll*.
253. Limacina helicina, *Phipps*.
254. Psyche globulosa, *Rang*.
255. Cleodora pyramidata, *Lin*.
256. Hyalea trispinosa, *Les*.

NUDIBRANCHIATA.

257. Limapontia zonata, *Grd*.
258. Placobranchus simplex, *Grd*.
259. Tergipes rupium, *Möll*.
260. Aeolis bostoniensis, *Couth*.
261. Aeolis farinacea, *Gould*.
262. Aeolis stellata, *Stm*.
263. Aeolis purpurea, *Stm*.
264. Aeolis diversa, *Couth*.
265. Aeolis gymnota, *Couth*.
266. Aeolis Olrikii, *Moerch*.
267. Aeolis salmonacea, *Couth*.
268. Aeolis mananensis, *Stm*.
269. Doto coronata, *Gmel*.
270. Dendronotus Reynoldsii, *Couth*.
271. Ancula sulphurea, *Stm*.
272. Proctaporia fusca, *O. Fabr*.
273. Polycera Holbollii, *Möll*.
274. Polycera illuminata, *Gould*.
275. Doris planulata, *Stm*.
276. Doris liturata, *Möll*.
277. Doris acutiuscula, *Stp*.
278. Doris obvelata, *Müll*.

OPISTHOBRANCHIATA.

279. Philine sinuata, *Stm*.
280. Philine quadrata, *Wood*.
281. Philine punctata, *Möll*.
282. Philine lineolata, *Couth*.
283. Scaphander puncto-striata, *M.*
284. Diaphana hiemalis, *Couth*.
285. Diaphana debilis, *Gould*.
286. Utriculus Gouldii, *Couth*.
287. Utriculus semen, *Reeve*.
288. Utriculus turritus, *Möll*.
289. Utriculus biplicatus, *Lea*.
290. Utriculus pertenuis, *Migh*.
291. Utriculus canaliculatus, *Say*.
292. Cylichna nucleola, *Reeve*.
293. Cylichna alba, *Brown*.
294. Cylichna oryza, *Tott*.
295. Bulla sculpta, *Reeve*.
296. Bulla incincta, *Migh*.
297. Bulla Reinhardtii, *Möll*.
298. Bulla solitaria, *Say*.
299. Tornatella puncto-striata,
C. B. Ad.

PROSOBRANCHIATA.

300. Chiton mendicarius, *Migh*.
301. Chiton apiculatus, *Say*.
302. Chiton cinereus, *Lin*.
303. Chiton marmoreus, *O. Fabr*.
304. Chiton laevis, *Penn*.
305. Chiton albus, *Lin*.
306. Amicula Emersonii, *Couth*.
307. Entalis striolata, *Stm*.
308. Entalis pliocena, *T. & II.*
309. Tectura testudinalis, *Müll*.
310. Tectura alveus, *Con*.
311. Lepeta caeca, *Müll*.
312. Pilidium rubellum, *O. Fabr*.
313. Crepidula unguiformis, *Lam*.
314. Crepidula fornicata, *Lin*.
315. Crepidula convexa, *Say*.
316. Crepidula aculeata, *Gm*.
317. Crucibulum striatum, *Say*.
318. Cemoria noachina, *Lin*.
319. Fissurella alternata, *Say*.
320. Clypidella pustula, *Lin*.
321. Janthina fragilis, *Brug*.
322. Scissurella crispata, *Flem*.
323. Adeorbis costulata, *Möll*.
324. Margarita minutissima, *Migh*.
325. Margarita helicina, *O. Fabr*.
326. Margarita Vahlii, *Möll*.
327. Margarita argentata, *Gould*.
328. Margarita Harrisoni, *Hancock*.
329. Margarita obscura, *Couth*.
330. Margarita acuminata, *Migh*.
331. Margarita varicosa, *Migh*.
332. Margarita cinerea, *Couth*.
333. Margarita groenlandica, *Ch*.
334. Trochus occidentalis, *Migh*.
335. Turbo crenulatus, *Gm*.
336. Cochliolepis parasitica, *Stm*.
337. Skenea planorbis, *Fabr*.
338. Rissoella? eburnea, *Stm*.
339. Rissoella? sulcosa, *Migh*.
340. Rissoa minuta, *Tott*.
341. Rissoa robusta, *Lea*.
342. Rissoa turriculus, *Lea*.
343. Rissoa latior, *Migh*.
344. Rissoa aculeus, *Gould*.
345. Rissoa saxatilis, *Möll*.
346. Rissoa multilineata, *Stm*.
347. Rissoa Mighelsii, *Stm*.
348. Rissoa castanea, *Möll*.
349. Rissoa exarata, *Stm*.
350. Rissoa carinata, *Migh*.
351. Rissoa scrobiculata, *Möll*.
352. Lacuna vincta, *Mont*.
353. Lacuna glacialis, *Möll*.

(c)

354. Lacuna neritoidea, *Gould.*
355. Littorina litorea, *Lin.*
356. Littorina palliata, *Say.*
357. Littorina rudis, *Mont.*
358. Littorina irrorata, *Say.*
359. Scalaria Humphreysii, *Kien.*
360. Scalaria turbinata, *Con.*
361. Scalaria lineata, *Say.*
362. Scalaria multistriata, *Say.*
363. Scalaria novangliae, *Couth.*
364. Scalaria groenlandica, *Perry.*
365. Acirsa borealis, *Beck.*
366. Solarium granulatum, *Lam.*
367. Vermetus radicula, *Stm.*
368. Caecum pulchellum, *Stm.*
369. Turritella erosa, *Couth.*
370. Turritella reticulata, *Migh.*
371. Turritella costulata, *Migh.*
372. Turritella acicula, *Stm.*
373. Aporrhais occidentalis, *Beck.*
374. Bittium arcticum, *Moerch.*
375. Bittium nigrum, *Tott.*
376. Bittium Greenii, *C. B. Ad.*
377. Triforis nigrocinctus, *C. B. Ad.*
378. Odostomia producta, *C. B. Ad.*
379. Odostomia fusca, *C. B. Ad.*
380. Odostomia dealbata, *Stm.*
381. Odostomia modesta, *Stm.*
382. Odostomia bisuturalis, *Say.*
383. Odostomia trifida, *Tott.*
384. Odostomia seminuda, *C. B. Ad.*
385. Odostomia impressa, *Say.*
386. Turbonilla interrupta, *Tott.*
387. Turbonilla nivea, *Stm.*
388. Menestho albula, *Möll.*
389. Obeliscus crenulatus, *Holmes.*
390. Eulima conoidea, *K. & S.*
391. Eulima oleacea, *K. & S.*
392. Velutina zonata, *Gould.*
393. Velutina haliotoides, *Müll.*
394. Velutina lanigera, *Möll.*
395. Velutina flexilis, *Mont.*
396. Marsenina micromphala, *Bergh.*
397. Marsenina groenlandica, *M.*
398. Onchidiopsis groenlandica, *B.*
399. Catinus perspectivus, *Say.*
400. Natica pusilla, *Say.*
401. Natica clausa, *Sow.*
402. Lunatia heros, *Say.*
403. Lunatia triseriata, *Say.*
404. Lunatia Gouldii, *Phil.*
405. Lunatia groenlandica, *Möll.*
406. Mamma? immaculata, *Tott.*
407. Mamma? nana, *Möll.*
408. Neverita duplicata, *Say.*

409. Bulbus flavus, *Gould.*
410. Amauropsis helicoides, *Johnst.*
411. Amaura candida, *Möll.*
412. Volva uniplicata, *Sow.*
413. Marginella roscida, *Redf.*
414. Mitra groenlandica, *Möll.*
415. Voluta junonia, *Chemn.*
416. Pleurotoma plicata, *C. B. Ad.*
417. Pleurotoma cerina, *K. & S.*
418. Pleurotoma bicarinata, *Couth.*
419. Mangelia rubella, *K. & S.*
420. Mangelia filiformis, *Holmes.*
421. Bela exarata, *Möll.*
422. Bela nobilis, *Möll.*
423. Bela turricula, *Mont.*
424. Bela Woodiana, *Möll.*
425. Bela harpularia, *Couth.*
426. Bela violacea, *Migh.*
427. Bela livida, *Möll.*
428. Bela decussata, *Couth.*
429. Bela Pingelii, *Möll.*
430. Bela cancellata, *Migh.*
431. Bela pleurotomaria, *Couth.*
432. Bela Vahlii, *Möll.*
433. Bela elegans, *Möll.*
434. Oliva litterata, *Lam.*
435. Olivella mutica, *Say.*
436. Columbella ornata, *Rav.*
437. Columbella avara, *Say.*
438. Columbella rosacea, *Gould.*
439. Columbella lunata, *Say*
440. Columbella dissimilis, *Stm.*
441. Dolium galea, *Lin.*
442. Semicassis granulosa, *Brug.*
443. Cassis cameo, *Stm.*
444. Pedicularia decussata, *Gould.*
445. Purpura lapillus, *Lin.*
446. Purpura floridana, *Con.*
447. Nassa obsoleta, *Say.* ⌞
448. Nassa trivittata, *Say.*
449. Nassa acuta, *Say.*
450. Nassa unicincta, *Say.*
451. Nassa vibex, *Say.*
452. Cerithiopsis terebralis, *C. B. A.*
453. Cerithiopsis Emersonii, *C. B. A.*
454. Acus dislocatus, *Say.*
455. Acus concavus, *Say.*
456. Buccinum undatum, *Lin.*
457. Buccinum cyaneum, *Brug.*
458. Buccinum ciliatum, *O. Fabr.*
459. Buccinum glaciale, *Lin.*
460. Buccinum Hancocki, *Moerch.*
461. Buccinum Donovani, *Gray.*
462. Buccinum undulatum, *Möll.*
463. Buccinum scalariforme, *Möll.*

464. Buccinum sericatum, *Hanc.*
465. Rapana? cinerea, *Say.*
466. Fusus norvegicus, *Chemn.*
467. Fusus pygmaeus, *Gould.*
468. Fusus pellucidus, *Hanc.*
469. Fusus propinquus, *Alder.*
470. Fusus Holbollii, *Möll.*
471. Fusus islandicus, *Chemn.*
472. Fusus ventricosus, *Gray.*
473. Fusus latericeus, *Möll.*
474. Fusus Kroyeri, *Möll.*
475. Fusus tornatus, *Gould.*
476. Fusus fornicatus, *O. Fabr.*
477. Fusus despectus, *Lin.*
478. Fusus decemcostatus, *Say.*
479. Trophon craticulatus, *O. Fabr.*
480. Trophon clathratus, *Lin.*
481. Trophon scalariformis, *Gould.*
482. Trophon Gunneri, *Loven.*
483. Sycotypus papyraceus, *Say.*
484. Busycon pyrum, *Dillw.*
485. Busycon canaliculatum, *Lin.*
486. Busycon carica, *Lin.*
487. Busycon perversum, *Lin.*
488. Trichotropis conica, *Möll.*
489. Trichotropis borealis, *B. & S.*
490. Admete viridula, *O. Fabr.*
491. Cancellaria reticulata, *Lin.*
492. Fasciolaria ligata, *Migh.*
493. Fasciolaria gigantea, *Kien.*
494. Fasciolaria tulipa, *Lin.*
495. Fasciolaria distans, *Lam.*
496. Ranella caudata, *Say.*
497. Murex spinicostata, *Val.*
498. Strombus alatus, *Gm.*

CEPHALOPODA.

499. Spirula fragilis, *Lam.*
500. Ommastrephes Bartramii, *Les.*
501. Onychia caribaea, *Les.*
502. Onychoteuthis Fabricii, *Möll.*
503. Onychoteuthis Bartlingii, *Les.*
504. Loligopsis pavo, *Les.*
505. Loligopsis hyperborea, *Stp.*
506. Sepiola atlantica, *D'Orb.*
507. Rossia palpebrosa, *Möll.*
508. Rossia Moelleri, *Stp.*
509. Loligo punctata, *DeKay.*
510. Loligo Pealei, *Les.*
511. Loligo brevipinna, *Les.*
512. Cirroteuthis Muelleri, *Esch.*

513. Octopus rugosus, *D'Orb.*
514. Octopus groenlandicus, *Dew.*

DOUBTFUL SPECIES.

515. Ascidia amphora, *Ag.*
516. Ascidia ocellata, *Ag.*
517. Arca improcera, *Con.*
518. Nucula radiata, *DeKay.*
519. Nucula cascoënsis, *Migh.*
520. Modiola pulex, *Lea.*
521. Modiola elliptica, *Lea.*
522. Modiola tulipa, *Lam.*
523. Modiola cicercula, *Möll.*
524. Mytilus faba, *O. Fabr.*
525. Lucina multistriata, *Con.*
526. Astarte Warhami, *Hanc.*
527. Venericardia cribraria, *Say.*
528. Cytherea occulta, *Say.*
529. Petricola dactylus, *Sow.*
530. Tellina tenuis, *Da Costa.*
531. Tellina versicolor, *Cozzens.*
532. Tellina maculosa, *Lam.*
533. Tellina mera, *Say.*
534. Doris pallida, *Ag.*
535. Dentalium occidentale, *Stm.*
536. Crepidula intorta, *Say.*
537. Crepidula acuta, *Lea.*
538. Infundibulum depressum, *Say*
539. Delphinula coarctata, *Migh.*
540. Margarita ornata, *DeKay.*
541. Margarita multilineata, *DeKay*
542. Cingula laevis, *DeKay.*
543. Cingula modesta, *Lea.*
544. Littorina lunata, *Lea.*
545. Turbo canaliculatus, *Say.*
546. Turritella areolata, *Stm.*
547. Turritella aequalis, *Say.*
548. Turritella alternata, *Say*
549. Chemnitzia spirata, *K. & S.*
550. Chemnitzia textilis, *Kurtz.*
551. Actaeon. parvus, *Lea.*
552. Pasithea sordida, *Lea.*
553. Sigaretus maculatus, *Say.*
554. Cerithium cancellatum, *Lea.*
555. Columbella spizantha, *Rav.*
556. Columbella Gouldiana, *Ag.*
557. Buccinum Wheatleyi, *DeKay.*
558. Buccinum zonale, *Lins.*
559. Fusus Trumbulli, *Lins.*
560. Fusus muricatus, *Mont.*

[SECOND EDITION.]

CHECK LIST

OF THE

SHELLS OF NORTH AMERICA.

TERRESTRIAL GASTEROPODA.

BY

W. G. BINNEY

List No. 1. The species of the Pacific coast from the extreme north to Mazatlan.

No. 2. The species of Eastern North America, from the boreal regions to the Rio Grande.

No. 3. The species found in Mexico exclusive of those included in No. 1 (viz. 3, 7, 8, 11, 23, 25, 35, 37, 39, 40, 41, 42, 43, 45, 46, 47) .

Section I.—PACIFIC COAST.

PULMONOBRANCHIATA.
Testacellidæ.
1. **Glandina Albersi,** *Pf.*
2. **Glandina turris,** *Pf.*
    Arionidæ.
3. **Arion foliolatus,** *Gld.*
    Helicidæ.
4. **Limax columbianus,** *Gld.*
5. **Succinea cingulata,** *Forbes.*
6. **Succinea Nuttalliana,** *Lea.*
7. **Succinea oregonensis,** *Lea.*
8. **Succinea rusticana,** *Gld.*
9. **Helix acutedentata,** *W. G. B.*
10. **Helix anachoreta,** *W. G. B.*
11. **Helix areolata,** *Pf.*
12. **Helix areolata,** *Pf.*
    var. β. *Pf.*
13. **Helix areolata,** *Pf.*
    var. γ. *Pf.*

14. **Helix arrosa,** *Gld.*
15. **Helix aspersa** *Mull.?*
16. **Helix californiensis,** *Lea.*
17. **Helix columbiana,** *Lea.*
18. **Helix cultellata,** *Thomson.*
19. **Helix devia,** *Gld.*
20. **Helix Dupetithouarsi,** *Desh.*
21. **Helix exarata,** *Pf.*
22. **Helix fidelis,** *Gray.*
23. **Helix germana,** *Gld.*
24. **Helix infumata,** *Gld.*
25. **Helix intercisa,** *W. G. B.*
26. **Helix Kelletti,** *Forb.*
27. **Helix levis,** *Pf.*
28. **Helix levis,** *Pf.*
    var. β. *Pf.*
29. **Helix loricata,** *Gld., Pf.*,
30. **Helix mazatlanica,** *Pf.*
31. **Helix mormonum,** *Pf.*

Section II.—Eastern North America.

117. Helix clausa, *Say.*
118. Helix concava, *Say.*
119. Helix Cooperi, *W. G. B.*
120. Helix cumberlandiana, *Lea.*
121. Helix demissa, *Binn.*
122. Helix dentifera, *Binn.*
123. Helix divesta, *Gld.*
124. Helix Dorfeuilliana, *Lea.*
125. Helix Edgariana, *Lea.*
126. Helix Edvardsi, *Bld.*
127. Helix egena, *Say.*
128. Helix electrina, *Gld.*
129. Helix elevata, *Say.*
130. Helix Elliotti, *Redf.*
131. Helix espiloca, *Bland.*
132. Helix exigua, *Stim.*
133. Helix exoleta, *Binn.*
134. Helix Fabricii, *Beck.*
135. Helix fallax, *Say.*
136. Helix fatigiata, *Say.*
137. Helix friabilis, *W. G. B.*
138. Helix fuliginosa, *Binn.*
139. Helix griseola, *Pf.*
140. Helix gularis, *Say.*
141. Helix gularis, *Say.*
    var. umbilicata.
142. Helix Gundlachi, *Pf.*
143. Helix Hazardi, *Bland.*
144. Helix Hindsi, *Pf.*
145. Helix hippocrepis, *Pf.*
146. Helix hirsuta, *Say.*
147. Helix hispida, *Linn.*
148. Helix hopetonensis, *Shut.*
149. Helix hortensis, *Mull.*
150. Helix incrustata, *Poey.*
151. Helix indentata, *Say.*
152. Helix indentata, *Say.*
    var. umbilicata.
153. Helix inflecta, *Say.*
154. Helix inornata, *Say.*
155. Helix interna, *Say.*
156. Helix interna, *Say.*
    var. albina.
157. Helix intertexta, *Binn.*
158. Helix intertexta, *Binn.*
    var. carinata.
159. Helix introferens, *Bland.*
160. Helix jejuna, *Say.*
161. Helix kopnodes, *W. G. B.*
162. Helix labyrinthica, *Say.*
163. Helix lævigata, *Pf.*
164. Helix lasmodon, *Phill.*
165. Helix leporina, *Gld.*
166. Helix ligera, *Say.*
167. Helix limatula, *Ward.*

168. Helix lineata, *Say.*
169. Helix major, *Binn.*
170. Helix maxillata, *Gld.*
171. Helix milium, *Morse.*
172. Helix minuscula, *Binn.*
173. Helix minutissima, *Lea.*
174. Helix Mitchelliana, *Lea.*
175. Helix monodon, *Rack.*
176. Helix monodon, *Rack.*
    var. 1. Helix fraterna, *Say.*
177. Helix monodon, *Rack.*
    var. 2. Helix Leaii, *Ward.*
178. Helix Mooreana, *W. G. B.*
179. Helix mordax, *Shutt.*
180. Helix multidentata, *Binn.*
181. Helix multilineata, *Say.*
182. Helix multilineata, *Say.*
    var. albina.
183. Helix multilineata, *Say.*
    var. rufa, unicolor.
184. Helix nitida, *Mull.*
185. Helix obstricta, *Say.*
186. Helix oppilata, *Mor.*
187. Helix Ottonis, *Pf.*
188. Helix palliata, *Say.*
189. Helix palliata, *Say.*
    var. carolinensis.
190. Helix pennsylvanica, *Green.*
191. Helix perspectiva, *Say*
192. Helix Postelliana, *Bld.*
193. Helix profunda, *Say.*
194. Helix pulchella, *Müll.*
195. Helix pulchella, *Müll.*
    var. costata.
196. Helix pustula, *Fer.*
197. Helix pustuloides, *Bld.*
198. Helix Roemeri, *Pf.*
199. Helix Rugeli, *Shutt.*
200. Helix Sayii, *Binn.*
201. Helix sculptilis, *Bld.*
202. Helix septemvolva, *Say.*
203. Helix solitaria, *Say.*
204. Helix spinosa, *Lea.*
205. Helix Steenstrupii, *Mörch.*
206. Helix stenotrema, *Fer.*
207. Helix striatella, *Anth.*
208. Helix subplana, *Binn.*
209. Helix suppressa, *Say.*
210. Helix tenuistriata, *Binn.*
211. Helix texasiana, *Mor.*
212. Helix texasiana, *Mor.*
    var. β, *Pf.*
213. Helix texasiana, *Mor.*
    var. .
214. Helix tholus, *W. G. B.*

4

215. Helix thyroides, *Say.*
216. Helix tridentata, *Say.*
217. Helix Troostiana, *Lea.*
218. Helix uvulifera, *Shutt.*
219. Helix varians, *Menke.*
220. Helix ventrosula, *Pf.*
221. Helix vortex, *Pf.*
222. Helix vultuosa, *Gld.*
223. Helix Wheatleyi, *Bland.*
224. Bulimus acicula, *Müller.*
225. Bulimus alternatus, *Say.*
226. Bulimus dealbatus, *Say.*
227. Bulimus decollatus, *Lin.*
228. Bulimus Dormani, *W. G. B.*
229. Bulimus floridanus, *Pf.*
230. Bulimus Gossei, *Pf.*
231. Bulimus gracillimus, *Pf.*
232. Bulimus harpa, *Say.*
233. Bulimus marginatus, *Say.*
234. Bulimus Mariæ, *Albers.*
235. Bulimus modicus, *Gld.*
236. Bulimus multilineatus, *Say.*
237. Bulimus octona, *Ch.*
238. Bulimus patriarcha, *W. G. B.*
239. Bulimus Schiedeanus, *Pf.*
240. Bulimus Schiedeanus, *Pf.*
    var. apice nigra.
241. Bulimus serperastrus, *Say.*
242. Bulimus subula, *Pf.*
243. Orthalicus undatus, *Brug.*
244. Orthalicus zebra, *Mull.*
245. Macroceramus Kieneri, *Pf.*
246. Achatina fasciata, *Müll.*
247. Achatina fasciata, *Mäll.*
    var. 1. Achatina crenata, *Sw.*
248. Achatina fasciata, *Müll.*
    var. 2. Achatina solida, *Say.*
249. Achatina lubrica, *Müll.*
250. Achatina picta, *Rve.*
251. Pupa armifera, *Say.*
252. Pupa badia, *Ad.*
253. Pupa contracta, *Say.*
254. Pupa corticaria, *Say.*
255. Pupa decora, *Gld.*
256. Pupa Hoppii, *Möll.*

257. Pupa incana, *Binn.*
258. Pupa pellucida, *Pf.*
259. Pupa pentodon, *Say.*
260. Pupa placida, *Say.*
261. Pupa rupicola, *Say.*
262. Pupa variolosa, *Gld.*
263. Vertigo Gouldii, *Binn*
264. Vertigo milium, *Gld.*
265. Vertigo ovata, *Say.*
266. Vertigo simplex, *Gld.*
267. Cylindrella Goldfussi, *Menke*
268. Cylindrella jejuna, *Gld.*
269. Cylindrella Poeyana, *Orb.*
270. Cylindrella Rœmeri, *Pf.*

Veronicellidæ.
271. Veronicella floridana, *Binn.*

Auriculidæ.
272. Melampus bidentatus, *Say.*
273. Melampus cingulatus, *Pf.*
274. Melampus coffea, *Linn.*
275. Melampus flavus, *Gmel.*
276. Melampus floridanus, *Shutt.*
277. Melampus obliquus, *Say.*
278. Melampus pusillus, *Gmel.*
279. Melampus Redfieldi, *Pf.*
280. Alexia myosotis, *Drap.*
281. Blauneria pellucida, *Pf.*
282. Leuconia Sayii, *Küst.*
283. Carychium exiguum, *Say.*

Truncatellidæ.
284. Truncatella bilabiata, *Pf.*
285. Truncatella caribæensis, *Sowb*
286. Truncatella pulchella, *Pf.*
287. Truncatella subcylindrica, *Gr.*

Cyclophoridæ.
288. Ctenopoma rugulosum, *Pf.*
289. Chondropoma dentatum, *Say.*

Helicinidæ.
290. Helicina chrysocheila, *Binn.*
291. Helicina Hanleyana, *Pf.*
292. Helicina occulta, *Say.*
293. Helicina orbiculata, *Say.*
294. Helicina subglobulosa, *Poey.*
295. Helicina tropica, *Pf.*

(e)

Section III.—MEXICO.

PULMONOBRANCHIATA.

Testacellidæ.

296. Glandina candida, *Shuttl.*
297. Glandina carminensis, *Mor.*
298. Glandina conularis, *Pf.*
299. Glandina cordovana, *Pf.*
300. Glandina corneola, *W. G. B.*
301. Glandina delicatula, *Shuttl.*
302. Glandina Ghiesbreghti, *Pf.*
303. Glandina indusiata, *Pfr.*
304. Glandina isabellina, *Pf.*
305. Glandina Liebmanni, *Pf.*
306. Glandina margaritacea, *Pf.*
307. Glandina monilifera, *Pf.*
308. Glandina nana, *Shuttl.*
309. Glandina pulchella, *Pf.*
310. Glandina orizabæ, *Pf.*
311. Glandina solidula, *Pf.?*
312. Glandina Sowerbyana, *Pf.*
313. Glandina speciosa, *Pf.*
314. Glandina stigmatica, *Shuttl.*
315. Glandina Vanuxemensis, *Lea.*

Helicidæ.

316. Vitrina mexicana, *Beck.*
317. Simpulopsis chiapensis, *Pf.*
318. Simpulopsis cordovana, *Pf.*
319. Simpulopsis Salleana, *Pf.*
320. Succinea brevis, *Dunker.*
321. Succinea undulata, *Say.*
322. Helix ariadnæ, *Pf.*
323. Helix Berlandieriana, *Mor.*
324. Helix bicincta, *Pf.*
325. Helix bicruris, *Pf.*
326. Helix bilineata, *Pf.*
327. Helix caduca, *Pf.*
328. Helix chiapensis, *Pf.*
329. Helix coactiliata, *Fer.*
330. Helix contortuplicata, *Beck.*
331. Helix cordovana, *Pf.*
332. Helix Couloni, *Shuttl.*
333. Helix flavescens, *Wiegm.*
334. Helix fulvoidea, *Mor.*
335. Helix Ghiesbreghti, *Nyst.*
336. Helix griseola, *Pf.*
337. Helix Guillarmodi, *Shuttl.*
338. Helix helictomphala, *Pf.*
339. Helix Hindsi, *Pf.*
340. Helix Humboldtiana, *Val.*
341. Helix implicata, *Beck.*

342. Helix lucubrata, *Say.*
343. Helix mexicana, *Koch.*
344. Helix oajacensis, *Koch.*
345. Helix plagioglossa, *Pf.*
346. Helix Salleana, *Pf.*
347. Helix stolephora, *Val.*
348. Helix tenuicostata, *Dunk.*
349. Helix texasiana, *Mor.*
350. Helix trypanompala, *Pf.*
351. Helix veracruzensis, *Pf.*
352. Helix zonites, *Pf.*
353. Bulimus alternatus, *Say.*
354. Bulimus attenuatus, *Pf.*
355. Bulimus aurifluus, *Pf.*
356. Bulimus cordovanus, *Pf.*
357. Bulimus coriaceus, *Pf.*
358. Bulimus costatostriatus, *Pf.*
359. Bulimus Droueti, *Pf.*
360. Bulimus Dunkeri, *Pf.*
361. Bulimus emeus, *Say.*
362. Bulimus fenestratus, *Pf.*
363. Bulimus gnomon, *Beck.*
364. Bulimus Gruneri, *Pf.*
365. Bulimus Hegewischi, *Pf.*
366. Bulimus Humboldti, *Rve.*
367. Bulimus livescens, *Pf.*
368. Bulimus Mariæ, *Albers.*
369. Bulimus Martensi, *Pf.*
370. Bulimus mexicanus, *Lam.*
371. Bulimus patriarcha, *W. G. Binn*
372. Bulimus punctatissimus, *Less.*
373. Bulimus rudis, *Anton.*
374. Bulimus Schiedeanus, *Pf.*
375. Bulimus serperastrus, *Say.*
376. Bulimus sulcosus, *Pf.*
377. Bulimus sulphureus, *Pf.*
378. Bulimus truncatus, *Pf.*
379. Bulimus varicosus, *Pf.*
380. Spiraxis acus, *Shuttl.*
381. Spiraxis auriculacea, *Pf.*
382. Spiraxis biconica, *Pf.*
383. Spiraxis catenata, *Pf.*
384. Spiraxis coniformis, *Shuttl.*
385. Spiraxis dubia, *Pf.*
386. Spiraxis euptycta, *Pf.*
387. Spiraxis irrigua, *Shuttl.*
388. Spiraxis lurida, *Shuttl.*
389. Spiraxis mitræformis, *Shuttl.*
390. Spiraxis Nicoleti, *Shuttl.*

391. Spiraxis nigricans, *Pf.*
392. Spiraxis oblonga, *Pf.*
393. Spiraxis parvula, *Pf.*
394. Spiraxis Shuttleworthi, *Pf.*
395. Spiraxis streptostyla, *Pf.*
396. Spiraxis turgidula, *Pf.*
397. Orthalicus Boucardi, *Pf.*
398. Orthalicus livens, *Pf.*
399. Orthalicus longus, *Pf.*
400. Orthalicus undatus, *Brug.*
401. Achatina ambigua, *Pf.*
402. Achatina chiapensis, *Pf.*
403. Achatina Rangiana, *Pf.*
404. Achatina trochlea, *Pf.*
405. Achatina trypanodes, *Pf.*
406. Cylindrella apiostoma, *Pf.*
407. Cylindrella arctospira, *Pf.*
408. Cylindrella attenuata, *Pf.*
409. Cylindrella Boucardi, *Pf.*
410. Cylindrella clava, *Pf.*
411. Cylindrella cretacea, *Pf.*
412. Cylindrella decollata, *Nyst.*
413. Cylindrella denticulata, *Pf.*
414. Cylindrella filicosta, *Shuttl.*
415. Cylindrella Ghiesbreghti, *Pf.*
416. Cylindrella goniostoma, *Pf.*
417. Cylindrella grandis, *Pf.*
418. Cylindrella Liebmanni, *Pf.*
419. Cylindrella mexicana, *Pf.*
420. Cylindrella Pfeifferi, *Menke.*
421. Cylindrella Pilocerei, *Pf.*
422. Cylindrella polygyra, *Pf.*
423. Cylindrella splendida, *Pf.*
424. Cylindrella teres, *Menke.*
425. Cylindrella turris, *Pf.*

Auriculidœ.

426. Melampus coffea, *Linn.*

Truncatellidœ.

427. Truncatella caribæensis, *Sowb.*

Cyclophoridœ.

428. Cyclotus Dysoni, *Pf.*
429. Cyclophorus Boucardi, *Sallé.*
430. Cyclophorus mexicanus, *M.*
431. Tudora planospira, *Pf.*
432. Cistula trochlearis, *Pf.*
433. Chondropoma cordovanum, *P.*
434. Chondropoma truncatum, *W.*

Helicinidœ.

435. Helicina brevilabris, *Pf.*
436. Helicina chiapensis, *Pf.*
437. Helicina chrysocheila, *Binn.*
438. Helicina chrysocheila, *Shuttl.*
439. Helicina cinctella, *Shuttl.*
440. Helicina concentrica, *Pf.*
441. Helicina cordilleræ, *Sallé.*
442. Helicina delicatula, *Shuttl.*
443. Helicina elata, *Shuttl.*
444. Helicina flavida, *Menke.*
445. Helicina Ghiesbreghti, *Pf.*
446. Helicina Heloisæ, *Sallé.*
447. Helicina Lindeni, *Pf.*
448. Helicina lirata, *Pf.*
449. Helicina merdigera, *Sallé.*
450. Helicina notata, *Salle.*
451. Helicina Oweniana, *Pf.*
452. Helicina Sandozi, *Shuttl.*
453. Helicina sinuosa, *Pf.*
454. Helicina tenuis, *Pf.*
455. Helicina tropica, *Pf.*
456. Helicina turbinata, *Wiegm.*
457. Helicina zephyrina, *Ducl.*
458. Schasicheila alata, *Mke.*
459. Schasicheila Nicoleti, *Shuttl.*
460. Schasicheila pannucea, *Mor.*

Proserpinidœ.

461. Ceres eolina, *Ducl.*
462. Ceres Salleana, *Gray.*

CHECK LIST

OF THE

SHELLS OF NORTH AMERICA.

FLUVIATILE GASTEROPODA.

BY

W. G. BINNEY.

THE species whose range is confined to Eastern North America are not indicated by any peculiar mark. The letter W. distinguishes those confined to the Pacific coast; the letters W. E. are affixed to the names of those found in both the Eastern and Western sections, while the Greenland and Mexican species are also respectively designated by the letters G. and M. This list has been compiled from all American publications and the few European monographs treating of this branch of the Mollusca. I have preferred giving the name of many doubtful species rather than omit that of any which my own limited knowledge of the subject does not lead me to consider a synonym. The list, therefore, is not offered as a complete elimination of the synonymy, but rather as a temporary guide to the arrangement of this portion of the collection. It should not be quoted as authority.

PECTINIBRANCHIATA.
Melaniidœ.
1. Melania abbreviata, *Anth.*
2. Melania abrupta, *Lea.*
3. Melania abscida, *Anth.*
4. Melania acuta, *Lea.*
5. Melania acuto-carinata, *Lea.*
6. Melania adusta, *Anth.*
7. Melania æqualis, *Hald.*
8. Melania alexandrensis, *Lea.*
9. Melania altipeta, *Anth.*
10. Melania altilis, *Lea.*
11. Melania alveare, *Conr.*
12. Melania ambusta, *Anth.*
13. Melania ampla, *Anth.*
14. Melania angulata, *Anth.*
15. Melania angulosa, *Menke.*
16. Melania angustispira, *Anth.*
17. Melania annulifera, *Conr.*
18. Melania approximata, *Hald.*
19. Melania arachnoidea, *Anth.*
20. Melania arctata, *Lea.*
21. Melania armigera, *Say.*
22. Melania assimilis, *Lea.*
23. Melania athleta, *Anth.*
24. Melania auriculæformis, *Lea.*
25. Melania auriscalpium, *Menke.*
26. Melania Babylonica, *Lea.*
27. Melania baculum, *Anth.*
28. Melania basalis, *Lea.*
29. Melania bella, *Conr.*
30. Melania bellacrenata, *Hald.*
31. Melania bicincta, *Anth.*
32. Melania bicolorata, *Anth.*
33. Melania bicostata, *Anth.*
34. Melania bitæniata, *Conr.*
35. Melania bizonalis, *DeKay.*
36. Melania blanda, *Lea.*

8

37. Melania Boykiniana, *Lea*.
38. Melania brevis, *Lea*.
39. Melania brevispira, *Anth*.
40. Melania Brumbyi, *Lea*.
41. Melania brunnea, *Anth*.
42. Melania Buddii, *Lea*.
43. Melania bulbosa, *Gld.* W.
44. Melania caliginosa, *Lea*.
45. Melania canaliculata, *Say*.
46. Melania cancellata, *Say*.
47. Melania carinata, *Rav.*
48. Melania carinifera, *Lam*.
49. Melania carino-costata, *Lea*.
50. Melania casta, *Anth*.
51. Melania castanea, *Lea*.
52. Melania catenaria, *Say*.
53. Melania catenoides, *Lea*.
54. Melania circinata, *Lea*.
55. Melania clara, *Anth*.
56. Melania Clarkii, *Lea*.
57. Melania clavæformis, *Lea*.
58. Melania cœlatura, *Conr*.
59. Melania cognata, *Anth*.
60. Melania columella, *Lea*.
61. Melania comma, *Conr*.
62. Melania compacta, *Anth*.
63. Melania concinna, *Lea*.
64. Melania congesta, *Conr*.
65. Melania conica, *Say*.
66. Melania consanguinea, *Anth*.
67. Melania coracina, *Anth*.
68. Melania corneola, *Anth*.
69. Melania coronilla, *Anth*.
70. Melania corpulenta, *Anth*.
71. Melania costata, *Rav*.
72. Melania costifera, *Hald*.
73. Melania costulata, *Lea*.
74. Melania crebri-costata, *Lea*.
75. Melania crebri-striata, *Lea*.
76. Melania crenatella, *Lea*.
77. Melania cristata, *Anth*.
78. Melania cubicoides, *Anth*.
79. Melania Curreyana, *Lea*.
80. Melania curta, *Hald*.
81. Melania curvata, *Lea*.
82. Melania curvilabris, *Anth*.
83. Melania cuspidata, *Anth*.
84. Melania cylindracea, *Conr*.
85. Melania decora, *Lea*.
86. Melania decorata, *Anth*.
87. Melania depygis, *Say*.
88. Melania Deshayesiana, *Lea*
89. Melania densa, *Anth*.
90. Melania dislocata, *Rav*.
91. Melania dubiosa, *Lea*.

92. Melania Duttoniana, *Lea*.
93. Melania ebenum, *Lea*.
94. Melania Edgariana, *Lea*
95. Melania elata, *Anth*.
96. Melania elegantula, *Anth*.
97. Melania elevata, *Say*.
98. Melania eliminata, *Anth*.
99. Melania elongata, *Lea*.
100. Melania exarata, *Menke*.
101. Melania exarata, *Lea*.
102. Melania excavata, *Anth*.
103. Melania excurata, *Conr*.
104. Melania exigua, *Conr.* W.
105. Melania exilis, *Hald*.
106. Melania eximia, *Anth*.
107. Melania expansa, *Lea*.
108. Melania fastigiata, *Anth*.
109. Melania filum, *Lea*.
110. Melania Florentiana, *Lea*.
111. Melania Foremani, *Lea*.
112. Melania formosa, *Conr*.
113. Melania fuliginosa, *Lea*.
114. Melania funebralis, *Anth*.
115. Melania furva, *Lea*.
116. Melania fuscata, *Desh*.
117. Melania fusiformis, *Lea*.
118. Melania fusco-cincta, *Anth*.
119. Melania gemma, *DeKay*.
120. Melania germana, *Anth*.
121. Melania gibbosa, *Lea*.
122. Melania gibbosa, *Raf.*
123. Melania glabra, *Lea*.
124. Melania glandula, *Anth*.
125. Melania glauca, *Anth*.
126. Melania globula, *Lea*.
127. Melania gracilior, *Anth*.
128. Melania gracilis, *Lea*.
129. Melania gracillima, *Anth*.
130. Melania gradata, *Anth*.
131. Melania grata, *Anth*.
132. Melania gravida, *Anth*.
133. Melania grisea, *Anth*.
134. Melania Haleiana, *Lea*.
135. Melania harpa, *Lea*.
136. Melania hastata, *Anth*.
137. Melania Haysiana, *Lea*
138. Melania Hildrethiana, *Lea*.
139. Melania Holstonia, *Lea*.
140. Melania hybrida, *Anth*.
141. Melania Hydeii, *Conr*.
142. Melania imbricata, *Anth*.
143. Melania impressa, *Lea*.
144. Melania incrassata, *Anth*.
145. Melania inemta, *Anth*.
146. Melania inflata, *Hald*.

(*f*)

147. Melania inflata, *Lea.*
148. Melania infrafasciata, *Anth.*
149. Melania inornata, *Anth.*
150. Melania intersita, *Hald.*
151. Melania intertexta, *Anth.*
152. Melania iostoma, *Anth.*
153. Melania iota, *Anth.*
154. Melania Jayana, *Lea.*
155. Melania Kirtlandiana, *Lea.*
156. Melania læta, *Jay.*
157. Melania lævis, *Lea.*
158. Melania laqueata, *Say.*
159. Melania latitans, *Anth.*
160. Melania Lecontiana, *Lea.*
161. Melania Liebmanni, *Phil.* **M.**
162. Melania ligata, *Menke.*
163. Melania livescens, *Menke.*
164. Melania lugubris, *Lea.*
165. Melania marginata, *Raf.*
166. Melania Menkeana, *Lea.* **W.**
167. Melania modesta, *Lea.*
168. Melania monozonalis, *Lea.*
169. Melania multilineata, *Say.*
170. Melania napilla, *Anth.*
171. Melania nassula, *Conr.*
172. Melania nebulosa, *Conr.*
173. Melania neglecta, *Anth.*
174. Melania Newberryi, *Lea.* **W.**
175. Melania niagarensis, *Lea.*
176. Melania nigrocincta, *Anth.*
177. Melania nigrina, *Lea.* **W.**
178. Melania nitens, *Lea.*
179. Melania nobilis, *Lea.*
180. Melania nodulosa, *Lea.*
181. Melania nucleola, *Anth.*
182. Melania oblita, *Lea.*
183. Melania obtusa, *Lea.*
184. Melania occidentalis, *Lea.*
185. Melania occulta, *Anth.*
186. Melania Ocoensis, *Lea.*
187. Melania oliva, *Lea.*
188. Melania olivula, *Conr.*
189. Melania opaca, *Anth.*
190. Melania oppugnata *Lea.*
191. Melania Ordiana, *Lea.*
192. Melania ovalis, *Lea.*
193. Melania ovoidea, *Lea.*
194. Melania ovularis, *Menke.*
195. Melania pagodiformis, *Anth.*
196. Melania pallescens, *Lea.*
197. Melania pallidula, *Anth.*
198. Melania paucicosta, *Anth.*
199. Melania perangulata, *Conr.*
200. Melania percarinata, *Conr.*
201. Melania perfusca, *Lea.*

202. Melania pernodosa, *Lea.*
203. Melania perstriata, *Lea.*
204. Melania pilula, *Lea.*
205. Melania picta, *Lea.*
206. Melania pinguis, *Lea.*
207. Melania planogyra, *Anth.* ˊ
208. Melania planospira, *Anth.*
209. Melania plebeius, *Anth.*
210. Melania plena, *Anth.*
211. Melania plicifera, *Lea.* **W.**
212. Melania pluristriata, *Say.* **M.**
213. Melania ponderosa, *Anth.*
214. Melania Postellii, *Lea.*
215. Melania Potosiensis, *Lea.*
216. Melania prasinata, *Conr.*
217. Melania producta, *Lea.*
218. Melania proscissa, *Anth.*
219. Melania proteus, *Lea.*
220. Melania proxima, *Say.*
221. Melania pulchella, *Anth.*
222. Melania pulcherrima, *Anth.*
223. Melania pumila, *Lea.*
224. Melania pupoidea, *Anth.*
225. Melania pyramidalis, *Mor.* **M**
226. Melania pyrenella, *Conr.*
227. Melania regularis, *Lea.*
228. Melania rhombica, *Anth.*
229. Melania rigida, *Anth.*
230. Melania robulina, *Anth.*
231. Melania robusta, *Lea.*
?32. Melania rubida, *Lea.* **M.**
233. Melania rufescens, *Lea.*
234. Melania rufula, *Hald.*
235. Melania rugosa, *Lea.*
236. Melania Saffordii, *Lea.*
237. Melania Schiedeana, *Phil.* **M**
238. Melania sculptilis, *Lea.*
239. Melania Sellersiana, *Lea.*
240. Melania semicarinata, *Say.*
241. Melania semicostata, *Conr.*
242. Melania shastaensis, *Lea.* **W.**
243. Melania silicula, *Gld.* **W**
244. Melania simplex, *Say.*
245. Melania solida, *Lea.*
246. Melania sordida, *Lea.*
247. Melania spinalis, *Lea.*
248. Melania spurca, *Lea.*
249. Melania striatula, *Lea.*
250. Melania strigosa, *Lea.*
251. Melania stygia, *Say.*
252. Melania subangulata, *Anth.*
253. Melania subcylindracea, *Lea*
254. Melania subglobosa, *Say.*
255. Melania subsolida, *Lea.*
256. Melania substricta, *Hald.*

257. Melania subularis, *Lea.*
258. Melania succinulata, *Anth.*
259. Melania sulcosa, *Lea.*
260. Melania symmetrica, *Conr.*
261. Melania symmetrica, *Hald.*
262. Melania tabulata, *Anth.*
263. Melania tæniolata, *Anth.*
264. Melania Taitiana, *Lea.*
265. Melania tecta, *Anth.*
266. Melania tenebro-cincta, *Anth.*
267. Melania tenebrosa, *Lea.*
268. Melania terebralis, *Lea.*
269. Melania teres, *Lea.*
270. Melania textilosa, *Anth.*
271. Melania torquata, *Lea.*
272. Melania torta, *Lea.*
273. Melania torulosa, *Anth.*
274. Melania tracta, *Anth.*
275. Melania trochiformis, *Conr.*
276. Melania Troostiana, *Lea.*
277. Melania tuberculata, *Lea.*
278. Melania turgida, *Lea.*
279. Melania uncialis, *Hald.*
280. Melania undosa, *Anth.*
281. Melania undulata, *Say.*
282. Melania valida, *Anth.*
283. Melania Vanuxemensis, *Lea.*
284. Melania varicosa, *Ward.*
285. Melania venusta, *Lea.*
286. Melania versipellis, *Anth.*
287. Melania vestita, *Conr.*
288. Melania vicina, *Anth.*
289. Melania virens, *Anth.*
290. Melania virgata, *Lea.*
291. Melania virginica, *Gmel.*
292. Melania viridis, *Lea.*
293. Melania viridula, *Anth.*
294. Melania vittata, *Anth.*
295. Melania vittata, *Raf.*
296. Melania wahlamatensis, *L. W.*
297. Melania Warderiana, *Lea. W.*
298. Melania zonalis, *Raf.*
299. Lithasia geniculata, *Hald.*
300. Lithasia lima, *Conr.*
301. Lithasia nuclea, *Lea.*
302. Lithasia nupera, *Say.*
303. Lithasia salebrosa, *Conr.*
304. Lithasia Showalterii, *Lea.*
305. Gyrotoma alabamensis, *Lea.*
306. Gyrotoma ampla, *Anth.*
307. Gyrotoma babylonica, *Lea.*
308. Gyrotoma Buddii, *Lea.*
309. Gyrotoma bulbosa, *Anth.*
310. Gyrotoma carinifera, *Anth.*
311. Gyrotoma castanea, *Lea.*

312. Gyrotoma constricta, *Lea.*
313. Gyrotoma costata, *Shuttl.*
314. Gyrotoma curta, *Mighels.*
315. Gyrotoma cylindracea, *Müll.*
316. Gyrotoma demissa, *Anth.*
317. Gyrotoma excisa, *Lea.*
318. Gyrotoma funiculata, *Lea.*
319. Gyrotoma glandula, *Lea.*
320. Gyrotoma glans, *Lea.*
321. Gyrotoma globosa, *Lea.*
322. Gyrotoma Hartmanii, *Lea.*
323. Gyrotoma incisa, *Lea*
324. Gyrotoma laciniata, *Lea.*
325. Gyrotoma ovalis, *Anth.*
326. Gyrotoma ovoidea, *Shuttl.*
327. Gyrotoma pagoda, *Lea.*
328. Gyrotoma pumila, *Lea.*
329. Gyrotoma pyramidata, *Shuttl.*
330. Gyrotoma quadrata, *Anth.*
331. Gyrotoma recta, *Anth.*
332. Gyrotoma robusta, *Anth.*
333. Gyrotoma salebrosa, *Anth.*
334. Gyrotoma Showalterii, *Lea.*
335. Gyrotoma virens, *Lea.*
336. Gyrotoma wetumpkaensis, *L*
337. Leptoxis affinis, *Hald.*
338. Leptoxis altilis, *Lea.*
339. Leptoxis ampla, *Anth.*
340. Leptoxis angulata, *Conr.*
341. Leptoxis Anthonyi, *Redfield.*
342. Leptoxis carinata, *Anth.*
343. Leptoxis carinata, *DeKay*
344. Leptoxis carinata. *Lea.*
345. Leptoxis carinifera, *Anth.*
346. Leptoxis cincinnatiensis, *Lea*
347. Leptoxis contorta, *Lea.*
348. Leptoxis corpulenta, *Anth.*
349. Leptoxis costata, *Anth.*
350. Leptoxis crassa, *Hald.*
351. Leptoxis crenata, *Hald.*
352. Leptoxis dentata, *Couthouy.*
353. Leptoxis dentata, *Lea.*
354. Leptoxis dilatata, *Conr.*
355. Leptoxis dissimilis, *Say.*
356. Leptoxis elegans, *Anth.*
357. Leptoxis flammata, *Lea.*
358. Leptoxis formosa, *Lea.*
359. Leptoxis Foremani, *Lea.*
360. Leptoxis fusca, *Hald. W.*
361. Leptoxis gibbosa, *Lea.*
362. Leptoxis Griffithiana, *Lea.*
363. Leptoxis incisa, *Lea.*
364. Leptoxis inflata, *Lea.*
365. Leptoxis integra, *Say.*
366. Leptoxis isogona, *Say.*

(*f*)

367. Leptoxis ligata, *Anth.*
368. Leptoxis littorina, *Hald.*
369. Leptoxis melanoides, *Conr.*
370. Leptoxis monodontoides, *Con.*
371. Leptoxis Nickliniana, *Lea.*
372. Leptoxis nigrescens, *Conr.*
373. Leptoxis Nuttalliana, *Lea.* W.
374. Leptoxis obovata, *Say.*
375. Leptoxis ornata, *Anth.*
376. Leptoxis patula, *Anth.*
377. Leptoxis picta, *Conr.*
378. Leptoxis pisum, *Hald.*
379. Leptoxis plicata, *Conr.*
380. Leptoxis prærosa, *Say.*
381. Leptoxis pumila, *Conr.*
382. Leptoxis Rogersii, *Conr.*
383. Leptoxis rubiginosa, *Lea.*
384. Leptoxis solida, *Lea.*
385. Leptoxis Showalterii, *Lea.*
386. Leptoxis squalida, *Lea.*
387. Leptoxis subglobosa, *Say.*
388. Leptoxis tæniata, *Conr.*
389. Leptoxis trilineata, *Say.*
390. Leptoxis trivittata, *DeKay.*
391. Leptoxis Troostiana, *Lea.*
392. Leptoxis tuberculata, *Lea.*
393. Leptoxis turgida, *Hald.*
394. Leptoxis variabilis, *Lea.*
395. Leptoxis virens, *Lea.* W.
396. Leptoxis viridula, *Anth.*
397. Leptoxis vittata, *Lea.*
398. Leptoxis zebra, *Anth.*
399. Io brevis, *Anth.*
400. Io fluvialis, *Say.*
401. Io inermis, *Anth.*
402. Io spinosa, *Lea.*
403. Io spirostoma, *Anth.*
404. Io tenebrosa, *Lea.*
405. Io turrita, *Anth.*

Viviparidæ.

406. Vivipara acuta, *Raf.*
407. Vivipara alleghanensis, *Gr.*
408. Vivipara angulata, *Lea.*
409. Vivipara castanea, *Müll.* G.
410. Vivipara castanea, *Val.*
411. Vivipara coarctata, *Lea.*
412. Vivipara contorta, *Shuttl.*
413. Vivipara coosaensis, *Lea.*
414. Vivipara cornea, *Val.*
415. Vivipara cyclostomatiformis, *Lea.*
416. Vivipara decapitata, *Anth.*
417. Vivipara decisa, *Say.*
418. Vivipara Elliotti, *Lea.*

419. Vivipara exilis, *Anth.*
420. Vivipara genicula, *Conr.*
421. Vivipara georgiana, *Lea.*
422. Vivipara gonula, *Raf.*
423. Vivipara Haleiana, *Lea.*
424. Vivipara humerosa, *Anth.*
425. Vivipara incrassata, *Lea.*
426. Vivipara integra, *Say.*
427. Vivipara intertexta, *Say.*
428. Vivipara lacustris, *Raf.*
429. Vivipara lima, *Anth.*
430. Vivipara magnifica, *Conr.*
431. Vivipara microstoma, *Kirtl.*
432. Vivipara multicarinata, *Hald.* M
433. Vivipara nitida, *Rav.*
434. Vivipara plaioxis, *Raf.*
435. Vivipara ponderosa, *Say.*
436. Vivipara scalaris, *Jay.*
437. Vivipara regularis, *Lea.*
438. Vivipara rudis, *Rav.*
439. Vivipara rufa, *Hald.*
440. Vivipara rugosa, *Raf.*
441. Vivipara subcarinata, *Say.*
442. Vivipara subglobosa, *Say.*
443. Vivipara subpurpurea, *Say.*
444. Vivipara subsolida, *Anth.*
445. Vivipara sulculosa, *Menke.*
446. Vivipara transversa, *Say.*
447. Vivipara Troostiana, *Lea.*
448. Vivipara verrucosa, *Raf.*
449. Vivipara vivipara, *Lin.*
450. Vivipara Wareana, *Shuttl*
451. Bithinia nuclea, *Lea.* W.
452. Bithinia seminalis, *Hinds.* W.
453. Bithinia tentaculata, *Lin.* G.
454. Valvata humeralis, *Say.* M.
455. Valvata pupoidea, *Gld.*
456. Valvata sincera, *Say.* W. E.
457. Valvata tricarinata, *Say.*
458. Ampullaria depressa, *Say.*
459. Ampullaria flagellata, *Say.* M.
460. Ampullaria malleata, *Jonas.* M.
461. Ampullaria paludinoides, *De Crist. et Jan.* M.
462. Ampullaria reflexa, *Sw.* M.
463. Ampullaria scalaris, *D'Orb.* M.
464. Ampullaria urceus, *Linn.?* M.
465. Ampullaria violacea, *Val.* M.
466. Amnicola attenuata, *Hald.*
467. Amnicola cincinnatensis, *A.*
468. Amnicola decisa, *Hald.*
469. Amnicola elongata, *Jay.*
470. Amnicola galbana, *Hald.*

(f)

471. Amnicola granum, *Say.*
472. Amnicola lapidaria, *Say.*
473. Amnicola limosa, *Say.*
474. Amnicola longinqua, *Gld.* **W.**
475. Amnicola lustrica, *Say.*
476. Amnicola Nickliniana, *Lea.*
477. Amnicola obtusa, *Lea.*
478. Amnicola orbiculata, *Lea.*
479. Amnicola pallida, *Hald.*
480. Amnicola parva, *Lea.*
481. Amnicola porata, *Say.*
482. Amnicola protea, *Gld.* **W.**
483. Amnicola tenuipes, *Couper.*
484. Amnicola Sayana, *Anth.*

PULMONOBRANCHIATA.
Limnæidæ.
485. Limnæa ampla, *Mighels.*
486. Limnæa apicina, *Lea.* **W.**
487. Limnæa appressa, *Say.*
488. Limnæa attenuata, *Say.* **M.**
489. Limnæa bulimoides, *Lea.* **W.**
490. Limnæa caperata, *Say.*
491. Limnæa casta, *Lea.*
492. Limnæa catascopium, *Say.*
       W. E.
493. Limnæa coarctata, *Lea.*
494. Limnæa columella, *Say.*
495. Limnæa curta, *Lea.*
496. Limnæa decollata, *Mighels.*
497. Limnæa desidiosa, *Say.*
498. Limnæa exigua, *Lea.* **W. E.**
499. Limnæa expansa, *Hald.*
500. Limnæa ferruginea, *Hald.* **W.**
501. Limnæa fusiformis, *Lea.*
502. Limnæa galbana, *Say.*
503. Limnæa gracilis, *Jay.*
504. Limnæa grœnlandica, *Beck.* **G.**
505. Limnæa Griffithiana, *Lea.*
506. Limnæa Haydeni, *Lea.*
507. Limnæa Holbollii, *Beck.* **G.**
508. Limnæa humilis, *Say.*
509. Limnæa jugularis, *Say.* **W. E.**
510. Limnæa Kirtlandiana, *Lea.*
511. Limnæa lanceata, *Gld.*
512. Limnæa lepida, *Gld.* **W.**
513. Limnæa megasoma, *Say.*
514. Limnæa obrussa, *Say.*
515. Limnæa pallida, *Ad.* **W. E.**
516. Limnæa palustris, *Lin.* **W. E.**
517. Limnæa parva, *Lea.*
518. Limnæa Pingelii, *Beck.* **G.**
519. Limnæa planulata, *Lea.*
520. Limnæa platyostoma, *Hald.*
521. Limnæa plica, *Lea.*

522. Limnæa proxima, *Lea.* **W.**
523. Limnæa reflexa, *Say.*
524. Limnæa rugosa, *Val.* **M.**
525. Limnæa rustica, *Lea.*
526. Limnæa solida, *Lea.* **W.**
527. Limnæa strigosa, *Lea.*
528. Limnæa subulata, *Dunk.* **M.**
529. Limnæa Vahlii, *Beck.* **G.**
530. Limnæa vitrea, *Hald.*
531. Pompholyx effusa, *Lea.* **W.**
532. Physa ancillaria, *Say.*
533. Physa aurantia, *Carp.* **W.**
534. Physa bullata, *Gld.* **W.**
535. Physa Charpentieri, *Küst.*
536. Physa concolor, *Hald.* **W.**
537. Physa distorta, *Hald.*
538. Physa elata, *Gld.* **W.**
539. Physa fragilis, *Mighels.*
540. Physa globosa, *Hald.*
541. Physa gyrina, *Say.*
542. Physa heterostropha, *Say.*
       W. E
543. Physa Hildrethiana, *Lea.*
544. Physa humerosa, *Gld.* **W.**
545. Physa hypnorum, *Lin.* **W. E**
546. Physa inflata, *Lea.*
547. Physa integra, *Hald.*
548. Physa mexicana, *Phil.* **M.**
549. Physa microstoma, *Hald.*
550. Physa nitens, *Phil.* **M.**
551. Physa osculans, *Hald.* **M.**
552. Physa Philippii, *Küster.*
553. Physa pomilia, *Conr.*
554. Physa semiplicata, *Küst.?*
555. Physa scalaris, *Jay.*
556. Physa solida, *Phil.*
557. Physa triticea, *Lea.*
558. Physa Troostiana, *Lea.*
559. Physa vinosa, *Gld.*
560. Physa virgata, *Gld.* **W.**
561. Physa virginea, *Gld.* **W.**
562. Planorbis albus, *Müll.*
563. Planorbis ammon, *Gld.* **W.**
564. Planorbis antrorsus, *Conr.*
565. Planorbis arcticus, *Beck.* **G.**
566. Planorbis armigerus, *Say.*
567. Planorbis bellus, *Lea.*
568. Planorbis bicarinatus, *Say.*
569. Planorbis Buchanensis, *Lea.*
570. Planorbis campanulatus, *Say.*
571. Planorbis corpulentus, *Say.*
       W. E
572. Planorbis deflectus, *Say.*
573. Planorbis dilatatus, *Gld.*
574. Planorbis exacutus, *Say.*

(f)

575. Planorbis fragilis, *Dunk.* **M.**
576. Planorbis glabratus, *Say.*
W. E.
577. Planorbis gracilentus, *Gld.* **W.**
578. Planorbis Haldemani, *D.* **M.**
579. Planorbis lentus, *Say.*
580. Planorbis Liebmanni, *D.* **M**
581. Planorbis multivolvis, *Case.*
582. Planorbis Newberryi, *Lea.* **W.**
583. Planorbis obtusus, *Lea.*
584. Planorbis opercularis, *Gld.* **W.**
585. Planorbis planulatus, *Cooper.*
W.
586. Planorbis parvus, *Say.*
587. Planorbis regularis, *Lea.*
588. Planorbis subcrenatus, *Carp.*
⸱ W.
589. Planorbis tenuis, *Phil.* **M.**
590. Planorbis Traskii, *Lea.* **W.**
591. Planorbis trivolvis, *Say.* **W. E.**

592. Planorbis trivolvis, *Say.*
var. fallax.
593. Planorbis tumens, *Carp.* **W.**
594. Planorbis tumidus, *Pf.* **M.**
595. Planorbis vermicularis, *Gld.*
W
596. Planorbis Wheatleyi, *Lea.*
597. Ancylus calcarius, *DeKay.*
598. Ancylus crassus, *Hald.* **W.**
599. Ancylus depressus, *Hald*
600. Ancylus diaphanus, *Hald.*
601. Ancylus elatior, *Anth.*
602. Ancylus filosus, *Conr.*
603. Ancylus fuscus, *Adams.*
604. Ancylus Newberryi, *Lea.* **W.**
605. Ancylus Nuttalli, *Hald.* **W.**
606. Ancylus obscurus, *Hald.*
607. Ancylus parallelus, *Hald.*
608. Ancylus patelloides, *Lea.* **W**
709. Ancylus rivularis, *Say.*
610. Ancylus tardus, *Say.*

(*f*)

CHECK LIST

OF THE

SHELLS OF NORTH AMERICA.

CYCLADES.

BY

TEMPLE PRIME.

[NOTE.—In the following list the species not marked are found living in the United States. F. signifies that they are found fossil. C. refers to Cuba; C. A. to Central America; H. to Honduras; J. to Jamaica; M. to Mexico; P. to Panama; Y. to Yucatan.]

1. Pisidium abditum, *Hald.*
2. Pisidium Adamsi, *Pr.*
3. Pisidium æquilaterale, *Pr.*
4. Pisidium arcuatum, *Pr.* **F.**
5. Pisidium compressum, *Pr.*
6. Pisidium contortum, *Pr.* **F.**
7. Pisidium ferrugineum, *Pr.*
8. Pisidium novi-eboraci, *Pr.*
9. Pisidium retusum, *Pr.* **H.**
10. Pisidium rotundatum, *Pr.*
11. Pisidium tenellum, *Gould.*
12. Pisidium variabile, *Pr.*
13. Pisidium ventricosum, *Pr.*
14. Pisidium virginicum, *Bgt.*

15. Sphærium acuminatum, *Pr.*
16. Sphærium aureum, *Pr.*
17. Sphærium bulbosum, *Anth.*
18. Sphærium cardissum, *Pr.*
19. Sphærium dentatum, *Hald.*
20. Sphærium eburneum, *Anth.*
21. Sphærium elevatum, *Hald.*
22. Sphærium emarginatum, *Pr.*
23. Sphærium fabale, *Pr.*
24. Sphærium flavum, *Pr.*
25. Sphærium fuscatum, *Rafin.*
26. Sphærium gracile, *Pr.*
27. Sphærium Jayanum, *Pr.*
28. Sphærium maculatum, *Mor.* **Y.**

29. Sphærium nobile, *Gould.*
30. Sphærium occidentale, *Pr.*
31. Sphærium partumium, *Say.*
32. Sphærium patellum, *Gould.*
33. Sphærium pygmeum, *Adams.* **J.**
34. Sphærium rhomboideum, *Say.*
35. Sphærium rosaceum, *Pr.*
36. Sphærium securis, *Pr.*
37. Sphærium solidulum, *Pr.*
38. Sphærium sphæricum, *Anth.*
39. Sphærium stamineum, *Conr.*
40. Sphærium striatinum, *Lam.*
41. Sphærium subtransversum, *Pr.*
   M
42. Sphærium sulcatum, *Lam.*
43. Sphærium tenue, *Pr.*
44. Sphærium tenuistriatum, *Pr.*
45. Sphærium transversum, *Say.*
46. Sphærium triangulare, *Say.* **M**
47. Sphærium truncatum, *Lin.*
48. Sphærium Veatleyii, *Adams.* **J.**

49. Cyrena californiensis, *Pr.*
50. Cyrena caroliniensis, *Lam.*
51. Cyrena cubensis, *Pr.* **C.**
52. Cyrena Cumingii, *Desh.* **C. A.**
53. Cyrena densata, *Conr.* **F.**
54. Cyrena floridana, *Conr.*
55. Cyrena insignis, *Desh.*

56. **Cyreua maritima,** *Adams.* **P.**
57. **Cyrena mexicana,** *Sowb.*
58. **Cyrena moreauensis,** *Meek &*
    Hayden. **F.**
59. **Cyrena nebraskensis,** *Pr.* **F.**
60. **Cyrena occidentalis,** *Meek &*
    Hayden. **F.**
61. **Cyrena olivacea,** *Cpr.* **C. A.**
62. **Cyrena panamensis,** *Pr.* **C. A.**

63. **Cyrena placens,** *Hanley.* **C. A.**
64. **Cyrena radiata,** *Hanley.* **C. A.**
65. **Cyrena salmacida,** *Morelet.* **C. A**
66. **Cyrena sordida,** *Hanley.* **C. A.**

67. **Corbicula convexa,** *Desh.* **C. A**
68. **Corbicula truncata,** *Pr.* **F.**
69. **Corbicula ventricosa,** *Pr* **M.**

(g)

CHECK LIST

OF THE

SHELLS OF NORTH AMERICA.

UNIONIDÆ.

BY

ISAAC LEA.

NORTH AMERICA.

Unionidæ.

1. Unio abacus, *Hald.*
2. Unio abbevillensis, *Lea.*
3. Unio Aberti, *Con.*
4. Unio acutissimus, *Lea.*
5. Unio æquatus, *Lea.*
6. Unio Æsopus, *Green.*
7. Unio affinis, *Lea.*
8. Unio aheneus, *Lea.*
9. Unio alatus, *Say.*
10. Unio altilis, *Con.*
11. Unio amœnus, *Lea.*
12. Unio amygdalum, *Lea.*
13. Unio angustatus, *Lea.*
14. Unio anodontoides, *Lea.*
15. Unio apicinus, *Lea.*
16. Unio apiculatus, *Say.*
17. Unio approximus, *Lea.*
18. Unio aquilus, *Lea.*
19. Unio aratus, *Lea.*
20. Unio arcæformis, *Lea.*
21. Unio arctatus, *Con.*
22. Unio arctior, *Lea.*
23. Unio arcus, *Con.*
24. Unio argenteus, *Lea.*
25. Unio arquatus, *Con.*
26. Unio asper, *Lea.*
27. Unio asperrimus, *Lea.*
28. Unio atrocostatus, *Lea.*
29. Unio atromarginatus, *Lea.*
30. Unio aureus, *Lea.*
31. Unio Bairdii, *Lea.*
32. Unio Baldwinensis, *Lea.*
33. Unio Barrattii, *Lea.*
34. Unio Barnesianus, *Lea.*
34a. Unio Bradleianus, *Lea.*
35. Unio biangulatus, *Lea.*
36. Unio biemarginatus, *Lea.*
37. Unio bigbyensis, *Lea.*
38. Unio Binneyi, *Lea.*
39. Unio Blandianus, *Lea.*
40. Unio Blandingianus, *Lea.*
41. Unio Bournianus, *Lea.*
42. Unio Boydianus, *Lea.*
43. Unio Boykinianus, *Lea.*
44. Unio bracteacus, *Gould.*
45. Unio brevidens, *Lea.*
46. Unio Brumbyanus, *Lea.*
47. Unio Buckleyi, *Lea.*
48. Unio Buddianus, *Lea.*
49. Unio bulbosus, *Lea.*
50. Unio Burkensis, *Lea.*
51. Unio buxeus, *Lea.*
52. Unio cacao, *Lea.*
53. Unio cælatus, *Con.*
54. Unio caliginosus, *Lea.*
55. Unio callosus, *Lea.*
56. Unio camelopardilis, *Lea.*
57. Unio camelus, *Lea.*
58. Unio camptodon, *Say.*
59. Unio canadensis, *Lea.*
60. Unio capax, *Green.*
61. Unio caperatus, *Lea.*
62. Unio capsæformis, *Lea.*
63. Unio cariosus, *Say.*
64. Unio castaneus, *Lea.*
65. Unio castus, *Lea.*
66. Unio catawbensis, *Lea.*
67. Unio chattanoogaensis, *Lea.*
68. Unio claibornensis, *Lea.*

69. Unio Clarkianus, *Lea.*
70. Unio clavus, *Lam.*
71. Unio cincinnatiensis, *Lea.*
72. Unio circulus, *Lea.*
73. Unio coccineus, *Lea.*
74. Unio collinus, *Con.*
75. Unio coloradoensis, *Lea.*
76. Unio compactus, *Lea.*
77. Unio compressus, *Lea.*
78. Unio compressissimus, *Lea.*
79. Unio complanatus, *Lea.*
80. Unio concavus, *Lea.*
81. Unio concestator, *Lea.*
82. Unio confertus, *Lea.*
83. Unio congaræus, *Lea.*
84. Unio Conradicus, *Lea.*
85. Unio constrictus, *Con.*
86. Unio contractus, *Lea.*
87. Unio contradens, *Lea.*
88. Unio Cooperianus, *Lea.*
89. Unio cor, *Con.*
90. Unio cornutus, *Bar.*
91. Unio coruscus, *Gould.*
92. Unio corvus, *Lea.*
93. Unio crassidens, *Lam.*
94. Unio creperus, *Lea.*
95. Unio crocatus, *Lea.*
96. Unio cumberlandianus, *Lea.*
97. Unio cuneolus, *Lea.*
98. Unio cuprinus, *Lea.*
99. Unio curtus, *Lea.*
100. Unio Cuvierianus, *Lea.*
101. Unio cylindricus, *Say.*
102. Unio cyrenoides, *Phili.*
103. Unio dactylus, *Lea.*
104. Unio dariensis, *Lea.*
105. Unio decisus, *Lea.*
106. Unio declivus, *Say.*
107. Unio decoratus, *Lea.*
108. Unio denigratus, *Lea.*
109. Unio discrepans, *Lea.*
110. Unio dispar, *Lea.*
111. Unio dolabriformis, *Lea.*
112. Unio dollabelloides, *Lea.*
112a. Unio dolosus. *Lea.*
113. Unio donaciformis, *Lea.*
114. Unio Dorfeuillianus, *Lea.*
115. Unio Downiei, *Lea.*
116. Unio dromas, *Lea.*
117. Unio Duttonianus, *Lea.*
118. Unio ebenus, *Lea.*
119. Unio Edgarianus, *Lea.*
120. Unio Eightsii, *Lea.*
121. Unio elegans *Lea.*
122. Unio Elliottii, *Lea.*

123. Unio ellipsis, *Lea.*
124. Unio Emmonsii, *Lea.*
125. Unio errans, *Lea.*
126. Unio Estabrookianus, *Lea.*
127. Unio exactus, *Lea.*
128. Unio excavatus, *Lea.*
129. Unio exiguus, *Lea.*
130. Unio extensus, *Lea.*
131. Unio fabalis, *Lea.*
132. Unio fallax, *Lea.*
133. Unio famelicus, *Gould.*
134. Unio fatuus, *Lea.*
135. Unio favosus, *Lea.*
136. Unio fibuloides, *Lea.*
137. Unio Fisherianus, *Lea.*
138. Unio flavescens, *Lea.*
139. Unio florentinus, *Lea.*
140. Unio floridensis, *Lea.*
141. Unio foliatus, *Hild.*
142. Unio folliculatus, *Lea.*
143. Unio Forbeseanus, *Lea.*
144. Unio Foremanianus, *Lea.*
145. Unio Forsheyi, *Lea.*
146. Unio fragosus, *Con.*
147. Unio fraternus, *Lea.*
148. Unio fucatus, *Lea.*
149. Unio fulgidus, *Lea.*
150. Unio fuliginosus, *Lea.*
151. Unio fulvus, *Lea.*
152. Unio fumatus, *Lea.*
153. Unio furvus, *Con.*
154. Unio fuscatus, *Lea.*
155. Unio Geddingsianus, *Lea.*
156. Unio geminus, *Lea.*
157. Unio Genthii, *Lea.*
158. Unio Georgianus, *Lea.*
159. Unio gibber, *Lea.*
160. Unio Gibbesianus, *Lea.*
161. Unio gibbosus, *Bar.*
162. Unio glaber, *Lea.*
163. Unio glans, *Lea.*
164. Unio globosus, *Lea.*
165. Unio Gouldii, *Lea.*
166. Unio gracilentus, *Lea.*
167. Unio gracilior, *Lea.*
168. Unio gracilis, *Barnes.*
169. Unio graniferus, *Lea.*
170. Unio Greenii, *Con.*
171. Unio Griffithianus, *Lea.*
172. Unio Haleianus, *Lea.*
173. Unio Hallenbeckii, *Lea.*
174. Unio Hanleyanus, *Lea.*
174a. Unio Hartmanianus, *Lea.*
175. Unio Haysianus, *Lea.*
176. Unio Hazlehurstianus, *Lea.*

286. Unio pallescens, *Lea.*
287. Unio palliatus, *Lea.*
288. Unio paludicolus, *Gould.*
289. Unio papyraceus, *Gould.*
289a. Unio parvulus, *Lea.*
290. Unio parvus, *Bar.*
291. Unio patulus, *Lea.*
292. Unio paulus, *Lea.*
293. Unio pectorosus, *Con.*
294. Unio pellucidus, *Lea.*
295. Unio penicillatus, *Lea.*
296. Unio penitus, *Con.*
297. Unio percoarctatus, *Lea.*
298. Unio perdix, *Lea.*
299. Unio permiscens, *Lea.*
300. Unio pernodosus, *Lea.*
301. Unio perovalis, *Con.*
302. Unio perovatus, *Con.*
303. Unio perpictus, *Lea.*
304. Unio perplexus, *Lea.*
305. Unio perplicatus, *Con.*
305a. Unio perpurpureus, *Lea.*
306. Unio perradiatus, *Lea.*
307. Unio personatus, *Say.*
308. Unio perstriatus, *Lea.*
309. Unio phaseolus, *Hild.*
310. Unio Phillipsii, *Con.*
311. Unio pictus, *Lea.*
312. Unio pilaris, *Lea.*
313. Unio pileus, *Lea.*
314. Unio pinguis, *Lea.*
315. Unio placitus, *Lea.*
315a. Unio plancus, *Lea.*
316. Unio planicostatus, *Lea.*
317. Unio Plantii, *Lea.*
318. Unio plenus, *Lea.*
319. Unio plicatus, *Lesueur.*
320. Unio pliciferus, *Lea.*
321. Unio Popeii, *Lea.*
322. Unio porrectus, *Con.*
323. Unio Postellii, *Lea.*
324. Unio Powellii, *Lea.*
325. Unio Prattii, *Lea.*
326. Unio Prevostianus, *Lea.*
327. Unio productus, *Con.*
328. Unio propinquus, *Lea.*
329. Unio proximus, *Lea.*
330. Unio pudicus, *Lea.*
331. Unio pulcher, *Lea.*
332. Unio pullatus, *Lea.*
333. Unio pullus, *Lea.*
334. Unio pulvinulus, *Lea.*
335. Unio pumilis, *Lea.*
336. Unio purpuratus, *Lam.*
337. Unio purpurellus, *Lea.*

338. Unio purpuriatus, *Say.*
339. Unio purus, *Lea.*
340. Unio pusillus, *Con.*
341. Unio pustulatus, *Lea.*
342. Unio pustulosus, *Lea.*
343. Unio Pybasii, *Lea.*
344. Unio pyramidatus, *Lea.*
345. Unio pyriformis, *Lea.*
346. Unio quadrans, *Lea.*
347. Unio quadratus, *Lea.*
348. Unio radians, *Lea.*
349. Unio radiatus, *Lam.*
350. Unio Raeensis, *Lea.*
351. Unio Rangianus, *Lea.*
352. Unio Ravenelianus, *Lea.*
353. Unio rectus, *Lam.*
354. Unio Reeveianus, *Lea.*
355. Unio regularis, *Lea.*
356. Unio retusus, *Lam.*
357. Unio Rhumphianus, *Lea.*
358. Unio roanokensis, *Lea.*
359. Unio rostriformis, *Lea.*
360. Unio Roswellensis, *Lea.*
361. Unio Rowellii, *Lea.*
362. Unio rubellinus, *Lea.*
363. Unio rufus, *Lea.*
364. Unio rufusculus, *Lea.*
365. Unio rotundatus, *Lam.*
366. Unio rubellus, *Con.*
367. Unio rubiginosus, *Lea.*
368. Unio rutersvillensis, *Lea.*
369. Unio rutilans, *Lea.*
370. Unio sagittiformis, *Lea.*
371. Unio salebrosus, *Lea.*
372. Unio satillaensis, *Lea.*
373. Unio satur, *Lea.*
374. Unio savannahensis, *Lea.*
375. Unio saxeus, *Con.*
376. Unio Schoolcraftensis, *Lea.*
377. Unio scitulus, *Lea.*
378. Unio securis, *Lea.*
379. Unio Shepardianus, *Lea.*
379a. Unio Showalterii, *Lea.*
380. Unio similis, *Lea.*
381. Unio simplex, *Lea.*
382. Unio simus, *Lea.*
383. Unio Sloatianus, *Lea.*
384. Unio solidus, *Lea.*
385. Unio sordidus, *Lea.*
386. Unio Sowerbianus, *Lea.*
387. Unio spadiceus, *Lea.*
388. Unio sparsus, *Lea.*
389. Unio spatulatus, *Lea.*
390. Unio spinosus, *Lea.*
391. Unio spissus, *Lea.*

392. Unio splendidus, *Lea.*
393. Unio stagnalis, *Con.*
394. Unio stapes, *Lea.*
395. Unio Stewardsonii, *Lea.*
396. Unio Stonensis, *Lea.*
397. Unio stramineus, *Con.*
398. Unio striatulus, *Lea.*
399. Unio striatus, *Lea.*
400. Unio strigosus, *Lea.*
401. Unio subangulatus, *Lea.*
402. Unio subcrassus, *Lea.*
403. Unio subcroceus, *Con.*
404. Unio subellipsis, *Lea.*
405. Unio subflavus, *Lea.*
406. Unio subgibbosus, *Lea.*
407. Unio subinflatus, *Con.*
408. Unio sublatus, *Lea.*
409. Unio subniger, *Lea.*
410. Unio subovatus, *Lea.*
411. Unio subplanus, *Lea.*
412. Unio subrotundus, *Lea.*
413. Unio subtentus, *Say.*
414. Unio succissus, *Lea.*
415. Unio sudus, *Lea.*
416. Unio sulcatus, *Lea.*
417. Unio symmetricus, *Lea.*
418. Unio tæniatus, *Con.*
419. Unio Taitianus, *Lea.*
420. Unio Tappanianus, *Lea.*
421. Unio tenebricus, *Lea.*
422. Unio tener, *Lea.*
423. Unio tenerus, *Rav.*
424. Unio tennesseensis, *Lea.*
425. Unio tenuissimus, *Lea.*
426. Unio tetralasmus, *Say.*
427. Unio tetricus, *Lea.*
428. Unio texasensis, *Lea.*
429. Unio Thorntonii, *Lea.*
430. Unio tortivus, *Lea.*
431. Unio trapezoides, *Lea.*
432. Unio triangularis, *Bar.*
433. Unio trigonus, *Lea.*
434. Unio Troostensis, *Lea.*
435. Unio Troschelianus, *Lea.*
436. Unio trossulus, *Lea.*
437. Unio tuberculatus, *Bar.*
438. Unio tuberosus, *Lea.*
439. Unio tumescens, *Lea.*
440. Unio Tuomeyi, *Lea.*
441. Unio turgidulus, *Lea.*
442. Unio turgidus, *Lea.*
443. Unio umbrans, *Lea.*
444. Unio umbrosus, *Lea.*
445. Unio undulatus, *Bar.*
446. Unio unicolor, *Lea.*

447. Unio utriculus, *Lea.*
448. Unio Vanuxemensis, *Lea.*
449. Unio varicosus, *Lea.*
450. Unio Vaughanianus, *Lea.*
451. Unio velatus, *Con.*
452. Unio ventricosus, *Bar.*
453. Unio venustus, *Lea.*
454. Unio verrucosus, *Bar.*
455. Unio verutus, *Lea.*
456. Unio vibex, *Con.*
457. Unio vicinus, *Lea.*
458. Unio virens, *Lea.*
459. Unio virescens, *Lea.*
460. Unio viridans, *Lea.*
461. Unio viridicatus, *Lea.*
462. Unio viridiradiatus, *Lea.*
463. Unio watereensis, *Lea.*
464. Unio Whiteianus, *Lea.*
465. Unio Woodwardianus, *Lea.*
466. Unio Zeiglerianus, *Lea.*
467. Unio zigzag, *Lea.*

468. Margaritana arcula, *Lea.*
469. Margaritana calceola, *Lea.*
470. Margaritana complanata, *Lea.*
471. Margaritana confragosa, *Lea.*
472. Margaritana connasaugaensis
    Lea.
473. Margaritana Curreyana, *Lea.*
474. Margaritana dehiscens, *Lea.*
475. Margaritana deltoidea, *Lea.*
476. Margaritana Elliottii, *Lea.*
477. Margaritana elliptica, *Lea.*
478. Margaritana etowahensis,
    Con.
479. Margaritana fabula, *Lea.*
480. Margaritana georgiana, *Lea.*
481. Margaritana Gesnerii, *Lea.*
482. Margaritana Hildrethiana, *Lea*
483. Margaritana holstonia, *Lea.*
484. Margaritana margaritifera,
    Lea. A. & P.
485. Margaritana marginata, *Lea.*
486. Margaritana minor, *Lea.*
486a. Margaritana quadrata, *Lea.*
487. Margaritana radiata, *Lea.*
488. Margaritana Raveneliana, *Lea.*
489. Margaritana rugosa, *Lea.*
490. Margaritana Spillmanii, *Lea.*
491. Margaritana tombigbeensis,
    Lea.
492. Margaritana triangulata, *Lea.*
493. Margaritana undulata, *Lea.*

494. Anodonta angulata, *Lea.*
495. Anodonta argentea, *Lea.*

496. Anodonta arkansensis, *Lea.*
497. Anodonta Benedictii, *Lea.*
498. Anodonta Buchanensis, *Lea.*
499. Anodonta californiensis,
    Lea. P.
500. Anodonta Couperiana, *Lea.*
501. Anodonta cultrata, *Gould.*
502. Anodonta cylindracea, *Lea.*
503. Anodonta Danielsii, *Lea.*
504. Anodonta dariensis, *Lea.*
505. Anodonta decora, *Lea.*
506. Anodonta denigrata, *Lea.*
507. Anodonta Dunlapiana, *Lea.*
508. Anodonta edentula, *Lea.*
509. Anodonta fragilis, *Lam.*
510. Anodonta ferruginea, *Lea.*
511. Anodonta Ferussaciana, *Lea.*
512. Anodonta fluviatilis, *Lea.*
513. Anodonta Footiana, *Lea.*
514. Anodonta Gesnerii, *Lea.*
515. Anodonta gibbosa, *Say.*
516. Anodonta gigantea, *Lea.*
517. Anodonta grandis, *Say.*
518. Anodonta Hallenbeckii, *Lea.*
519. Anodonta harpethensis, *Lea.*
520. Anodonta horda, *Gould.*
521. Anodonta imbecillis, *Say.*
522. Anodonta implicata, *Say.*
524. Anodonta Kennerlyi, *Lea.*
525. Anodonta lacustris, *Lea.*

526. Anodonta Lewisii, *Lea.*
527. Anodonta Linnæana, *Lea.*
528. Anodonta lugubris, *Say.*
529. Anodonta Marryatana, *Lea.*
530. Anodonta modesta, *Lea.*
531. Anodonta Nuttalliana, *Lea.* P
532. Anodonta oblita, *Lea.*
533. Anodonta opaca, *Lea.*
534. Anodonta oregonensis, *Lea.* P.
535. Anodonta ovata, *Lea.*
536. Anodonta papyracea, *Anth.*
537. Anodonta pavonia, *Lea.*
538. Anodonta pepiniana, *Lea.*
539. Anodonta plana, *Lea.*
540. Anodonta plicata, *Hald.*
541. Anodonta salmonia, *Lea.*
542. Anodonta Shafferiana, *Lea.*
542a. Anodonta Showalterii, *Lea.*
543. Anodonta Stewartiana, *Lea.*
544. Anodonta subcylindracea,
    Lea.
545. Anodonta suborbiculata, *Say.*
546. Anodonta subvexa, *Con.*
547. Anodonta tetragona, *Lea.*
548. Anodonta texasensis, *Lea.*
549. Anodonta virens, *Lea.*
550. Anodonta virgulata, *Lea.*
551. Anodonta wahlamatensis,
    Lea. P.
552. Anodonta Wardiana, *Lea.*

MEXICO AND CENTRAL AMERICA.

1. Unio aratus, *Lea.* Nicaragua.
2. Unio Averyi, *Lea.* Isth. Darien.
3. Unio aztecorum, *Lea.* Mexico.
4. Unio Berlandierii, *Lea.* Mexico.
5. Unio Caldwellii, *Lea.* Is. Darien.
5a. Unio cognatus, *Lea.*
5b. Unio Couchianus, *Lea.*
6. Unio cuprinus, *Lea.* Mexico.
7. Unio cyrenoides, *Phili.* Nicarag.
8. Unio discus, *Lea.* Mexico.
9. Unio Dysonii, *Lea.* Honduras.
10. Unio goascoranensis, *Lea.* Hon.
11. Unio Liebmanni, *Phili.* Mexico.
12. Unio manubius, *Gould.* Mexico.
13. Unio medellinus, *Lea.* Mexico.
14. Unio mexicanus, *Phili.* Mexico.
15. Unio Newcombianus, *Lea.* Nic.
16. Unio Nicklinianus, *Lea.* Mexico.
17. Unio persulcatus, *Lea.* Mexico.
18. Unio petrinus, *Gould.* Mexico.
19. Unio pliciferus, *Lea.* Mexico.
20. Unio Poeyanus, *Lea.* Mexico.

21. Unio Rowellii, *Lea.* Cent. Amer.
21a. Unio Saladoensis, *Lea.*
22. Unio sapotalensis, *Lea.* Mexico.
23. Unio scamnatus, *Morelet.* Cuba.
24. Unio semigranosus, *Vondem-*
    Busch, Mexico.
25. Unio tabascoensis, *Phili.* Mex.
26. Unio tampicoensis, *Lea.* Mex.
27. Unio tecomatensis, *Lea.* Mex.
28. Unio umbrosus, *Lea.* Mexico.
29. Anodonta cylindracea, *Lea.*
30. Anodonta glauca, *Valen.* Mex.
31. Anodonta globosa, *Lea.* Mex.
32. Anodonta Henryana, *Lea.* Mex.
33. Anodonta Holtonis, *Lea.* New
    Grenada.
34. Anodonta luteola, *Lea.* Is. Dar.
35. Anodonta montezuma, *Lea.*
    Central America.
36. Anodonta nicaragua, *Phili.*
    Nicaragua.